the seems
the glitch in sleep

the Seems
the glitch in sleep

John Hulme and Michael Wexler

illustrations by Gideon Kendall

BLOOMSBURY
CHILDREN'S
BOOKS

Published by Bloomsbury U.S.A. Children's Books
175 Fifth Avenue, New York, NY 10010
Distributed to the trade by Holtzbrinck Publishers

Library of Congress Cataloging-in-Publication Data
Hulme, John.
The glitch in sleep / by John Hulme and Michael Wexler.
p.   cm. — (The Seems ; bk. 1)
Summary: When twelve-year-old Becker Drane is recruited by The Seems, a parallel
universe that runs everything in The World, he must fix a disastrous glitch in the
Department of Sleep that threatens the ability of everyone to ever fall asleep again.
ISBN-13: 978-1-59990-129-9 • ISBN-10: 1-59990-129-3
[1. Sleep—Fiction.   2. Technology—Fiction.   3. Space and time—Fiction.]
I. Wexler, Michael.   II. Title.
PZ7.H8844G1 2007   [Fic]—dc22   2007002598

First U.S. Edition 2007
Typeset by Westchester Book Composition
Printed in the U.S.A. by Quebecor World Fairfield
2   4   6   8   10   9   7   5   3   1

All papers used by Bloomsbury U.S.A. are natural, recyclable products
made from wood grown in well-managed forests. The manufacturing processes
conform to the environmental regulations of the country of origin.

To Everyone Who Believed

Contents

DEPARTMENT OF LEGAL AFFAIRS, THE SEEMS

Non-Disclosure Agreement (NDA)
[Form #1504-3]

TO WHOM IT MAY CONCERN:

I. THE FOLLOWING INFORMATION TO BE REPRINTED
HEREIN, WITH REFERENCE TO OR INDEMNIFICATION OF
THE SEEMS, ANY OF ITS DEPARTMENTS, SUBSIDIARIES,
ACTIVITIES, MACHINERIES, EMPLOYEES, EFFECTS UPON
THE WORLD, OR PECULIARS OR SPECIFICS HEREIN, IS THE
EXPRESS WRITTEN PROPERTY OF THE SEEMS, AND ANY
REPUBLICATION, RETRANSMISSION, RECONVERSATION,
REPROMULGATION, REGURGITATION, OR RECAPITULATION
ENACTED BY ANY READER OF THIS TEXT IS HEREBY
PROHIBITED, RECOMMENDED AGAINST, SEVERELY
DISCOURAGED, OUTLAWED, BANNED, AND FORBIDDEN.
IN OTHER WORDS, KEEP IT TO YOURSELF.

II. THE FOLLOWING INFORMATION TO BE REPRINTED HEREIN
AND IN FACT IS REPRINTED HEREIN ALBEIT *PRIMA FACIE A PRIORI*
TRUE, IS, CAN, AND WILL BE SOLELY INDEMNIFIED BY FACT OF
THE SEEMS AND ALL SUBSIDIARY RIGHTS ARE SUBJECT TO
DEFINITION REQUIRING THE EXPRESS WRITTEN CONSENT
OF SEEMS SUBSIDIARY OR THOSE THEREIN REQUITED. ALL AND
ANY INFORMATION REPUBLISHED HEREIN IS AND WILL BE
MUTUALLY DENIED OR REMANDED BY FORCE AND RECOGNIZES
ITSELF TO BE SUCH. AS FORBIDDEN UNDER RULE 643B, CODE 7,
PARAGRAPH 4, LINES 8–15 OF THE RULEBOOK, COPYRIGHT
SEEMSBURY PRESS, XXMBVJII.

III. ALL DEPARTMENTS, TOOLS, NAMES, LOCATIONS, DIRECTIONS,
CAREERS, JOB CHOICES, INFORMATION ABOUT THE WORLD AND THE
FUNCTIONING OF THE WORLD, THE INNER WORKINGS, FIXERS, BRIEFERS,
THE SEEMS, THE TRUE NATURE OF THE UNIVERSE, THE POWERS THAT BE,

THE RELATIVE BENEVOLENCE OR MALEVOLENCE OF THE PLAN, ANY HISTORICAL INFORMATION, PAST MISSIONS, FUTURE IMPLICATIONS, AND EXPLANATIONS OF THE WAY THINGS WORK ARE HEREBY INTENDED AND RELEASED ONLY (!) TO THE UNDERSIGNED INDIVIDUAL WHO POSSESSES THIS TEXT.

SIGNATURE OF THIS DOCUMENT BINDS THE SIGNATOR TO THE UNBRIDLED CONFIDENTIALITY OF THE SEEMS OR, SHOULD THEY REPEAT THE INFORMATION BARED HEREIN, ANY AND ALL RETALIATION BY THE POWERS THAT BE AND SEEMSIAN ENTITIES MAY BE ENFORCED. SUCH **PENALTIES** FOR THE UNSPECIFIED RELEASE OF SENSITIVE SEEMSIAN INFORMATION INCLUDE, BUT ARE NOT LIMITED TO, REMOVAL OF L.U.C.K., CEASING OF BIG IDEAS, WITHHOLDING OF SLEEP, DENIAL OF CERTAIN PUBLIC WORK SPECTACLES, LACK OF OVERSIGHT BY CASE WORKER, DOWNGRADING OF THREAD IMPORTANCE WITHIN CHAIN-OF-EVENT CONSTRUCTION, ETC.

IV. THIS DOCUMENT IS DRAFTED BY THE LEGAL AFFAIRS DEPARTMENT OF THE SEEMS AND IS VALID UNDER THE LAWS THEREIN. BY AGREEING TO THIS DOCUMENT, YOU WILL BE PRIVY TO INFORMATION NOT PRIVY TO OTHERS, HOWEVER NO OTHER GOVERNING BODY, COURT, LEGAL SERVICE, STATUTE, WRIT, OR CERTIFICATE OF HABEUS CORPUS WILL BE ALLOWABLE IN THE COURT OF PUBLIC OPINION. TO MAKE A LONG STORY SHORT: THIS DOCUMENT SUPERSEDES ALL LAWS OF THE WORLD FOR NOW AND IN PERPETUITY UNTIL THE END OF TIME, SHOULD IT OCCUR, OR NOT.

V. THESE INCIDENCES, SHOULD THEY OCCUR, CARRY WITH THEM DOUBLE PENALTIES INCLUDING, BUT NOT LIMITED TO, TIME SERVED IN SEEMSBERIA, COMMUNITY SERVICE IN THE FLAVOR MINES, OR COMPLETE REHABILITATION, PER ORDER BY THE COURT OF PUBLIC OPINION, ESQ.

X _____

SIGNATURE OF READER

_____

DATE

Preface

Ever since the beginning of Time, people have endeavored to understand what makes The World tick. How does it work? Where did it come from? And most of all, who built it in the first place?

Charles Darwin had a theory, which he called "evolution." Plato told his students it was just a play of shadows on the wall. And Buddha said that life is suffering, so you might as well have fun.

Confucius, Galileo, Black Elk, Einstein, Jung, Al-Kindi—prophets and visionaries all—each of whom contributed to the greater understanding of The World we live in today.

Unfortunately, all of them were wrong.

High Pressure

Village of Covas, Minho, Portugal

The sun beat mercilessly on Alvarro Gutierrez as he reached down and let the parched earth slip through his fingers. All around him the soil was dry and lifeless, his crops browned and withering.

"*Dame la barra que adivina, Sancho.*" (Give me the divining rod, Sancho.)

Alvarro's six-year-old son handed him the ancient twig that was naturally the shape of a fork. The farmer gripped the ends and held them close to his body, then extended the stem outward and performed the time-honored ritual of divination. He knew in his heart that the rumors of an underground spring were just that—rumors—but he had to try something. Or else . . .

"Nothing." Alvarro tossed the stick aside in disgust. "There is nothing there."

Sancho's eyes fell to the ground.

"What are we going to do, Poppa?"

Alvarro gathered himself, for he knew it scared Sancho to see him so beaten. He still hoped to pass this land on to the boy someday, as his father had done to him, and his father before that. All told, this farm had been home to the Gutierrez family for nine generations, but if another harvest was lost, the shared dreams of his ancestors would come to an end with him.

"Don't worry, Sancho. The rain will come." Alvarro forced a smile. "You'll see, the rain will come."

But the sky was clear and blue.

Rain Tower, Department of Weather, The Seems

Becker Drane had barely stepped onto the roof of the sky-scraper, when the Station Chief was already in his face.

"You're late." The supervisor's tie was undone and sweat beaded off his brow. "Didn't they tell you to get here ASAP?"

"I'm sorry—there was nothing I could do."

This was the truth, but the details were too embarrassing to share. Becker had been stuck at Rachel Adler's bat mitzvah at The Pines Manor and there was no way to get away without being spotted by a rabbi or chaperone. But that was no excuse, especially at a time like this.

"Is my Fixer here yet?"

"Already up top, with three of my best men."

Becker glanced skyward. An elevator shaft led high into the air and ended at the top of a gigantic wooden water tower.

Stenciled on the side in fading blue paint was the hallowed symbol of this department—clouds parting in front of a radiant sun.

"Hurry up, kid," begged the Chief. "If we don't get this back online, we're gonna have another Gobi on our hands!"

Without a second thought, Becker was locking the cage of the rickety lift and pushing the lever toward "Up." At twelve years, six months, and eleven days, he was the youngest Briefer on the Duty Roster, but that did not exempt him from the rigors of the job. Today, he had been called into Weather because a large amount of Rain Water earmarked for the Iberian Peninsula had failed to reach its destination, and the cause remained unknown. In situations such as these, a specialist was called in—a member of an elite corps, who could get the job done when no one else could.

They were known as Fixers.

The lift arrived with a rusty clank and Becker stepped onto the top of the Tower. He was not yet a Fixer by any means, but being a Briefer was the next best thing. It required two years of Training in and of itself, and gave one the distinct honor of being a Fixer's right-hand man (or woman).

"Over here!"

Up ahead, four figures stood huddled in the mist. Three were Weathermen—crack meteorologists wearing Badges with the same insignia as the Tower—and the fourth, a twentysomething girl, with double-braided pig-tails and flip-flops on her feet.

"Glad you could make it, Briefer Drane."

7

Great. If matters weren't bad enough already, the Fixer assigned to this Mission was Cassiopeia Lake.

"Yes, sir. I mean, ma'am. I mean, sir. Sorry I'm late."

Back in The World, "Casey" worked at a surf shop in Australia, but here in The Seems, she was practically a living legend. Becker had only met her a few times before, but he had studied her career in great detail—all Briefers had, because most of them either wanted to *be* Casey Lake or had a major crush on her. (Or both.)

"Stuck at White Castle again, mate?"

"Yessir—Sliders were tasty." Becker breathed a sigh of relief because she didn't seem to be pissed. "What's the 411?"

"Not sure yet. The boys were just filling me in."

At the feet of the Weathermen was an open manhole that led into the cavernous tank below. This was the same Tower that held all of the World's precious Rain, and it was closely guarded to ensure the water within was kept both safe and clean.

"At first we thought it was just a Dry Spell . . ." Weatherman #1 tried to keep his cool. "But when we ran a diagnostic, the sensors reported nothing was leaving the tank."

"This is bad, man. This is really bad!"

Weathermen #2 and #3 were younger (and hipper) than the more straight-laced #1, and though they had big ideas for the future of Weather, they were not as experienced in the clutch.

"If we don't fix the problem soon," shouted #3, "Sectors 48 to 60 could be parched forev—"

"Relax," said Casey, taking control. "How far down to the water?"

"Could be a ways," reported #1, "we're almost at the end of the Rainy Season."

Casey reached into her messenger bag, which was embroidered with the logo of the Fixers—a double-sided wrench inside a circle. Inside that bag were all the Tools one would ever need, but all she pulled out this time was a small black stone. A few long seconds later, a distant splash could be heard in the darkness below.

"Never a dull moment." She smiled mischievously at Becker. Only Casey Lake could be psyched about making a free-fall jump of this magnitude, with no clue of what was waiting at the bottom.

But that's why she was the best.

SPLASH!

When Becker's stomach returned to its rightful home, he was submerged in icy-cold rainwater. Fortunately, both of them had brought along their standard-issue wetsuits, which kept them warm as they prepared to dive below.

"You okay?" asked Casey, spit-cleaning the window of her mask.

"Yeah, that was awesome," claimed Becker, but in truth, he was still shaking from the plunge. He had to pull himself together, though, for there was still a body of water beneath them the size of a lake. "You hear that?"

A vibration rippled through the Rain, along with a mechanical *thrum* from somewhere down below.

"Sounds like the Regulator Pump," surmised Casey. "We'd better get down there quick."

Becker nodded, and bit down on his mouthpiece hard. Though he had been on sixteen Missions before, this one had come through with a Degree of Difficulty of 8.2 and the Dispatcher had mentioned the distinct possibility of foul play.

"Stay frosty," warned Fixer Lake before she dropped beneath the surface.

"Staying frosty, sir."

With flashlight in hand, he followed her down into the murky depths.

By the time they reached the bottom, the pressure was intense, yet that was the least of their concerns. The Regulator Pump— a hydraulic turbine built into the floor—was doing its best to churn out Rain, but the water wasn't going anywhere. And it wasn't difficult to see why.

Someone had jammed a giant cork into the drainpipe that led to The World.

"Maybe we should call for backup?" asked Becker over the intercom.

"No time," said Casey. "Recommendation?"

Back in the Day, Briefers had merely been in charge of delivering the Mission Report ("briefing" the Fixer), but since then, the job had evolved. Now they also handled small repairs, Tool recommendations, and general assistance in all its various and sundry forms.

"Corkscrew™[1]?" Becker suggested.

---

1. All Tools copyright the Toolshed, the Institute for Fixing & Repair (IFR), The Seems, XVUIVV (All Rights Reserved).

"Agreed."

From inside her Toolkit, Casey pulled out a metal contraption, which unfolded to become nearly six feet tall. It was the old-fashioned kind, silver, with the two extending arms (not the newfangled kind that do all the work for you) and it took all of their combined strength to manually drill the bit into the cork. But with each grunting twist, the screw sank deeper and the mechanical arms rose higher, like a swimmer preparing to dive.

"Slow down," said Casey, when they'd reached the halfway point. "The minute this thing comes free, the water's gonna move pretty fas—"

"Did you see that?"

A large chunk of cork had broken off from the screw, and Becker thought he'd caught a glimpse of something that broke away with it. He swam over to take a closer look, and sure enough, there it was—a tiny glass capsule bobbing along the bottom of the tank.

"What do you got?" asked Casey.

Becker picked up the tube and looked inside. There was a piece of paper, rolled up like a scroll.

"Looks like a note."

As he cautiously removed the rubber stopper, the first hint of concern spread across Casey's face.

"Be careful. Somebody put that there so we would find it."

In all truth, Becker should have seen it coming. Yes, he'd read the memo about an increase in Booby Traps and no, he didn't miss the slight tingling on the back of his neck, but on that night he was still a Briefer and not as in tune with his 7th

Sense as he someday would be. So it caught him completely by surprise when he unwrapped the message to see what was printed inside:

BOOM.

"Casey, look out—"

But it was too late.

"What was that?"

Back at topside, the ground was still shaking, and Weathermen #2 and #3 had begun to freak.

"The whole Tower's gonna blow!"

"And once that happens it's game over, man! Game over!"

But Weatherman #1 had been through a number of Tropical Depressions, Winter Storm Warnings, and other hard nights like this (which is why he'd been promoted to Weatherman #1).

"Don't worry, Freddy. They'll Fix it."

He placed a reassuring hand on #3's shoulder.

"They always do."

When Becker came to, the first thing he saw was his Briefcase, floating aimlessly a few feet out of reach. His head was still spinning, and he felt as if he were stuck in a Dream—the same horrible nightmare he had had so many times in Training, where he had blown a Mission that cost The World dearly. But when he saw the shattered wood on the bottom of the tank, everything came back in a flash.

The cork had been packed with explosives, cued to detonate after the capsule came free. The force of the blast had sent Becker tumbling, while Casey and what remained of the cork were driven straight up toward the surface, where they had vanished in the gloom.

"Drane to Fixer Lake, come in! Drane to Fixer Lake!"

Nothing but static.

"Casey, you okay?"

Still nothing. Even if she had survived the explosion, chances were she was out of commission. But there was no time to go in search of the Fixer, for the Mission had taken a terrible turn.

Just as Casey had predicted, the removal of the cork combined with the buildup in pressure had caused a devastating whirlpool. Water was rushing down through the drain, straight toward Sectors 48 to 60, and though that might seem like a good thing, it was in fact quite the opposite. With nothing to control the flow, the entire World's supply of Rain could be dumped on southern Europe in a single burst—unleashing a deluge that hadn't been seen since the days of the Great Flood.[2] There was no one left to stop the disaster other than Becker Drane, and he had to do it now.

But how? The mouth of the pipe had been torn asunder, and there was nothing in his Briefcase designed for this task. The only remnant of their earlier efforts—the Corkscrew—had

---

2. For more on "The Great Flood," please see: *Classic Blunders of The Seems (Or Were They Intentional?)* by Sitriol B. Flook (copyright XVIUJNN, Seemsbury Press).

been nailed to the floor by the force of the current. And yet . . . something about the way its arms extended over the drain triggered a vague idea. An image was coming into focus—a picture of simple but masterful engineering—that he must have seen somewhere in Training. Or maybe in his own—

Becker was swimming toward the whirlpool before he'd even formulated a plan. From inside his Briefcase, he produced two odd-shaped items, neither of which seemed appropriate to the operation at hand. The first was a section of chain about six feet long—excess slack from a Gear of Time he'd greased a few weeks back—and the other, a lid from a Barrel of Fun. When clamped to the leverlike arms of the 'Screw, it added up to a makeshift version of the same remarkable device he'd seen with his mind's eye: the inner workings of a toilet bowl.

Becker tentatively extended the lid, attempting to use it like the flapper in his commode, but he badly underestimated the strength of the rushing water. It yanked him off balance, then quickly pulled him under the lid and into the drainage hole. Somehow he managed to keep a vicious grip on the chain, but with the weight of a million gallons of water bearing down upon him, it was only a matter of time before the Briefer was sucked down the sluice pipe, and into the In-Between.

It's true what they say about that moment before you die—a flood of images passing through your mind—and Becker was no exception. He thought about the Mission and how at least he could take some solace in the fact that as soon as he let go, the rubber lid would close above him and surely save The World. He remembered Training, and what a bummer it would be that after everything he'd been through, he would never make it to Fixer. But most of all, he saw the faces of his family. He wondered how they would be notified and if they would be okay.

Becker's arms had finally given out when from nowhere, a hand appeared on his wetsuit and started pulling him from the hole. It was connected to an arm, which was adjoined to a shoulder, which was the property of a girl with double-braided pigtails that he was more than happy to see.

"Somebody call a plumber?"

"You did it!" cried #3, helping to pull the Briefer and Fixer out of the water. "By the infinite wonder that lies at the heart of the Plan, you did it!"

Sure enough, Becker's contraption had restored control of the Rain Tower to the Weathermen, who were already jerry-rigging a way to operate it via a host of ropes and pulleys.

"It's not over yet, mates," reminded Casey, as she tended to the burns on her shoulders and arms. "We've still gotta cross our i's and dot our t's."

She finished wrapping a bandage, then turned to Becker, who was still on his knees coughing up water.

"How you holdin' up?"

He nodded, then held something up in the air.

"Take a look at this."

In Becker's hand was the glass tube that had been hidden in the cork. It was empty, save for a strange image etched onto the side—the image of a cresting wave—and Casey nodded solemnly, for she knew exactly what it meant.

The Tide had struck again.

Village of Covas, Minho, Portugal

"Papi!"

Alvarro Gutierrez turned to see his wife, Maria, walking toward him from the house, their infant daughter in her hands.

"Mr. Ramirez from the bank just called again. He wants to know if we've come to a decision?"

Alvarro looked to his son and to the baby, who giggled and cooed, too young to understand—then finally back up to his wife. In the eyes of his beloved, he was searching for hope, but all he found were tears instead.

"Tell Señor Ramirez that we will never sell this land!" He grabbed his family and pulled them close.

"Never!"

On a hill overlooking the farm, two mysterious figures gazed down upon the scene. Their hair was soaking wet.

"Isn't it a little suspicious?" asked Becker.

"Don't you believe in Miracles, Briefer Drane?"

Casey pulled her Receiver™ off her belt. It was orange, with a retractable wire. She dialed #624.

"Lake to Weather Station, come in."

The voice of Weatherman #1 came back.

"Weather Station here. We read you loud and clear . . ."

"Okay, then let's start it slow." Casey scanned the surrounding countryside, the cloudless sky above. "Vague but palpable, volume 4."

"Vague but palpable, 4." The way he yelled it, you could tell

#1 was shouting directions to someone else, and a moment later, a faint rumble could be heard in the distance.

"Nice," said Casey, psyched. "Now roll it this time, with a slight clap on the end."

The Gutierrez family was trudging back to their house when the first rumble froze them in their tracks. Now they stood together, as a second sound sent chills down their spines.

Thunder, rolling toward them, with a slight clap on the end.

Casey nodded her head in satisfaction. For her, this is what Fixing was all about.

"Cue the clouds!"

The sound of a few switches being thrown piped over her Receiver, before #1 echoed the command.

"Cue the clouds!"

As the family looked up in wonder, a dark shadow moved across their faces. Somewhere in the distance, a dog began to bark, and a flash of lightning split a tree.

The flash had just faded when Casey shouted into her Receiver, "Another one! And don't hit anything this time!"

"Georgie, the yellow lever, not the blue!"

High above, another bolt streaked through the blackening sky.

"Now?" asked #1, ready to deliver the goods.

"Stand by."

"Standing by."

If there was one thing Becker admired about Casey, it was her patience. She never seemed in a hurry to get anywhere, which is probably why she always got there right on time.

"Annnnnnnnddddddddd . . . HIT IT!"

A thick drop of water landed on the arid ground, just missing the foot of Alvarro Gutierrez. And so did another. Maria and Sancho held out their hands, unable to believe their eyes, but it was true. Rain began to fall in buckets, showering every inch of the thirsty land.

As the water dripped from their faces, the family burst into tears, hugging each other as one.

Amid the torrential downpour, Becker and Casey looked down upon the farm below. The dog had joined the family, jumping around and barking, and it was hard not to share in the joy.

"Nice work, boys."

"She says nice work!" A tumult of cheers piped through the Receiver.

"Now low pressure for at least a week and then it's up to you."

"My pleasure!" shouted #1 with satisfaction. For him and his crew, this was what Weather was all about.

"Lake, out."

Casey hung up and sat down beside her Briefer. All around the hillside, there were other farms and other celebrations.

"Do you think there'll be a Rainbow?" asked Becker.

"I don't know. That's up to the Department of Public Works."

Becker nodded, pretending to act like he already knew that. There were so many departments and sub-departments in The Seems, it was hard to remember who did what sometimes.

"Slim Jim?"

He offered Casey his traditional post-Mission treat, and she looked at it curiously before taking a bite.

"Nice maneuver down there by the cork."

"You saw that?" Becker tried to conceal his pleasure. (You have to understand, Casey Lake was like "the man." Except she was a girl.) "It was just L.U.C.K.[3]"

"The residue of Design." She laughed, and he couldn't argue with that.

Below them, the screen door to the Gutierrez home swung shut and the jubilation had begun. Their farm had been saved . . . and their future along with it.

"Let me ask you something, Briefer Drane."

"Yeah?"

"How many Fixers are there in The World?"

Becker thought it might be a trick question, but he couldn't figure out the trick, so he gave the answer that everybody knew.

"Exactly thirty-six, if you include Tom Jackal."

Casey waited just long enough before smiling again and delivering the news that every Briefer dreams to hear . . .

"I think I'm looking at #37."

---

3. See Appendix A: "Glossary of Terms."

The Best Job in The World

Becker Drane's life wasn't always this exciting. Before he got his position in The Seems, he was just a regular kid in a regular town with a pretty regular life. Every day he attended school at Irving Elementary, rode his bike to practice for the second-to-last place Deli King Soccer team, and spent the rest of his time as the (mostly) dutiful son of Dr. and Mrs. Dr. F. B. Drane, who lived at 12 Grant Avenue, Highland Park, New Jersey.

It really wasn't a bad existence. He had lots of friends and a good skateboard, and all the video games / comic books / baseball cards that anyone could ever want. Yet even though everything was fine and he wasn't an orphan or anything like that, Becker couldn't shake the feeling that there was something . . . missing.

Until that day in Chapter 1.

Chapter 1 Books & Café, Highland Park, New Jersey—Three Years Ago

"BD—your hot choco's up!"

Becker looked up from his homework to see his mug of piping hot cocoa sitting on the counter.

"Be right there, Rick."

Rick was working the counter today, which was always a good sign. "You want some whipped cream on that?"

"Yeah, make it a double."

As the barista put the finishing touches on the towering mound, Becker was thankful for the break from biology. While the inner workings of a paramecium were fascinating to some, he didn't have plans to be a scientist or a microorganism anytime soon, and the spring weather outside beckoned for kickball or a further exploration of the Cleveland Avenue woods.

"Can you put it on my tab? I think I'm a little bit short."

"You got it, man. Just get me back next time."

That was the great thing about Chapter 1. There was a Starbucks just a few blocks away, but Chapter 1 just had a special kind of vibe. It was located practically in the living room of someone's house and was generally frequented by grad students, writers, artists, and local personalities, all of whom Becker considered his friends.

The third grader grabbed his hot chocolate and reclaimed his favorite window perch, which gave views of both outside and inside the shop. Big Mike and Kenny were sitting at their usual table, locked in another epic battle on the chessboard, while on the plush velvet couch, Eve and Efrem were still in their ongoing two-year debate about the films of some guy named Tarkovsky. This was par for the course, but over on the announcements table, something caught Becker's eye that he had never seen before.

Wedged between the self-published poetry chapbooks and the schedule for open-mic night was a small, nondescript white box, with a piece of paper taped to the front. It said:

APPLY HERE FOR THE BEST JOB IN THE WORLD

"Hey, Rick! What's that box all about?"

"Who knows? People put all kinds of stuff on that table."

Becker finished the last dollop of whipped cream and headed for a closer look. Next to the box was a Dixie cup filled with miniature No. 2 pencils, along with a stack of applications. Though he was only nine years old at the time and not in dire need of employment, Becker couldn't resist picking up the form.

SEEMSIAN APTITUDE TEST
This questionnaire will test, in shape, size, and dimension, your aptitude for a position in The Seems.

Becker had no idea what The Seems was nor what this job entailed, but unlike most tests, this one seemed kind of fun. So he began to fill it out.

Name: F. Becker Drane
Address: 12 Grant Ave., Highland Park, NJ, 08904
Telephone (optional): (Becker never gave out his cell)

Other than that, there were only three questions on the exam:

Question 1: Are you a little bored with life? Not that you're unhappy, but have you always had this nagging feeling in the back of your mind that maybe you were meant to do something more?

That was weird. This is exactly what Becker had been feeling lately, but he had never really put it into words. The answer was either:

_____ YES or _____ NO

Question 2: If there was a Tear in the Fabric of Reality and you were called in to handle the job, which Tool would you employ?

A. _____ A Rounded Scopeman 4000™
B. _____ A Boa Constrictor XL™
C. _____ A needle and thread
D. _____ I have no idea

Next to each of the tool suggestions were diagrams, as if they had been reprinted from a technical manual. And last but not least:

Question 3: Pretend The World was being remade from Scratch and you were in charge. What kind of world would you create?

Any normal person would have put this test down right away, assuming it was a lark or an experiment for somebody's psychology dissertation, but Becker had always been the kind of person who thought about such things. He scribbled his answer to Question #3 and by the time he was finished, the entire thing was a mélange of pictures, arrows, and charts. But as he folded it up into a square and dropped it in the slot, he never imagined it would amount to anything at all.

Eight months later, Highland Park was hit with what came to be known as "the Blizzard to end all Blizzards." Unbeknownst to the locals, this was actually an offensive by the Department of Weather, which had been under a great deal of criticism for having "gone soft." So to prove they still had the moxie, the giant red button on the Snow Blower had been pressed for the first time in a long time, and their pride and reputation were promptly restored.

Meanwhile, Grant Avenue had been transformed into a winter wonderland, the perfect setting for the age-old blood feud between the Drane/Crozier clan and the loathsome Hutkin boys. Snowballs had been hurled. Trees shaken to cause avalanche. And many precious lives lost in a cause worth fighting for. (Not really.)

"See ya later, Con-Man."

"Later, Drane-O."

As the survivors straggled home to drink hot chocolate and lick their wounds, Becker lingered for a few extra clicks. There was no telling if hostilities would break out tomorrow, so he wanted to be sure the D/C arsenal was replenished, should battle once again ensue.

"Hey, Becks—heads up!"

Becker turned just in time to see a blob of white smash him in the face.

"Ow! You are so dead!"

Becker picked up a snowball of his own and hurled it (inaccurately) at Amy Lannin, who was laughing hysterically across the street. Amy was the only kid from Lawrence Avenue who was allowed to play on Grant, mostly because she was an incredibly accurate snowball chucker, but also because she was Becker's best friend.

"Where were you when I needed you? I almost got turned into a Popsicle today!"

"Sorry. Ballet class. I have to be a girl sometimes, y'know . . ."

"Well, not tomorrow, I hope. We need to get revenge."

"Revenge? I love revenge. It's a dish best eaten cold." She chucked another one, purposely missing him by the slimmest of margins. "I'll meet you at the weapons depot, 11:00 a.m. sharp."

"Deal."

As Amy skipped home, Becker staggered back to his own house at #12 Grant. He hoped his mom hadn't started dinner yet, because after all this hard work, he had developed a craving for a baked ziti from Highland Pizza.

"Mr. Drane?"

Becker turned to see a man in a suit and paisley tie, carrying a briefcase and walking toward him.

"Mr. F. Becker Drane?"

The guy was rather underdressed for winter, with no jacket, hat, or gloves to speak of. Becker had nothing against talking to strangers—how else were you going to meet new people?—but enough admonitions from his mom, dad, local law enforcement, and school assemblies had made him somewhat wary.

"Who wants to know?"

"Allow me to introduce myself." The man handed him a business card. "Nick Dejanus, Associate Director of Human Resources."

According to the card, Dejanus worked for a company called The Seems. The Seems? Where had he heard that name before? But before he could ask, the man started to shiver.

"Is winter always this cold?"

"Not always," replied Becker. "Global warming's kind of taken the bite out of things."

"Global Warming! Don't even get me started. If Nature doesn't get their act together, I assure you heads will roll!"

"Ever think about wearing a coat?" asked the boy.

"My wife thought I should 'fully' experience The World this time." The man rolled his eyes, clearly regretting the decision. "But at least the nearest Door is right around the corner."

"Door to where?"

"I'm sorry. You'd think after four years on the job I would know how to do this already." He reached into his briefcase and pulled out a laminated piece of eight-and-a-half-by-eleven-inch paper, covered in scribbles, arrows, and charts. "Is this your handwriting?"

Becker looked at the sloppy mess.

"Yep. That's me."

And that's when it all came back to him. The box at Chapter 1. The Seemsian Aptitude Test and "The Best Job in The World." But that had been months ago and he hadn't heard a thing.

"Then on behalf of the Powers That Be, I would like to extend you an invitation to become a Candidate at the Institute for Fixing & Repair." Before Becker could ask what that was, the man handed him an oversized envelope with the same four-color logo that was printed on his card.

"Orientation begins tomorrow at 8:00 a.m. and Fixer Blaque is very punctual, so I wouldn't be late."

Becker stood there in the snow with the packet in his hands, mystified.

"Smile, kid," Dejanus said, turning and heading back to wherever he had come from. "Your application was accepted!"

Becker went home, and after a shower and some much-needed R & R, he unsealed the packet and examined the materials within. Packed neatly in bubble wrap were three distinct items: some kind of temporary ID card, a pair of what appeared to be ski goggles, and an offer letter, explaining to him the nature of the opportunity at hand.

According to the letter, The World he lived in wasn't actually what he thought it was—it was something much, much better. And should he accept the offer, he would have a chance not only to find out what The World *really* was but to join the team responsible for keeping it safe. To be honest, Becker didn't believe a word of it, but it did sound kind of cool. There were specific directions inside pinpointing the location of the nearest Door, via which he could attend the Orientation.

As Fate would have it, the next day was a snow day, and with a few hours to spare before his meeting with Amy, Becker considered the offer more seriously. Of course, there was the prospect of going to an undisclosed location at the behest of a strangely dressed man, which would have sent chills up the spines of every parent and educator in Highland Park. But Becker was his own man, and believed strongly in his street smarts and ability to escape from any potential hazard—though he brought along a little "protection" just in case.

That morning, he got on his bike, picked up a bacon, egg, and cheese sandwich from the Park Deli, and followed the directions to the back of Cleveland Avenue. This part of town was a strange netherworld—a cross between warehouse-type businesses, doctor's offices, a small chocolate factory, and a marshland of thickets and weeds. According to the packet, the so-called Door was somehow located at the very back of Illuminating Experiences: Becker's friend Connell Hutkin's mother's second husband Bernie's lighting company, which had gone out of business not three years ago.

"Hello—anybody there?" Becker checked the fresh powder and saw one set of footprints leading to and from the abandoned plant. "You should know that I am heavily armed and extremely dangerous."

No response except the wind and the tinkling of icicles in the trees.

Becker proceeded with caution, placing his hand on the Chinese star in his back pocket (the one he'd gotten at the Route 1 flea market before it got turned into a multiplex), and followed the footsteps around to the back. There was a stairway here that led down to a single black door, which looked suspiciously like the entrance to the basement or boiler room.

"If I'm not home in an hour, the police know where I am!"

Again, nothing but the wind in the weeds.

He threw another peek over his shoulder, then started the short but slow trip to the bottom of the stairs. The Door itself was still covered in snow, but when he wiped it off he was shocked to see the same logo that was printed on his packet—except faded and weathered from time. There was a swipe pad next to it and, following the instructions, Becker took out the temporary ID and slid it straight across. For a second there was no reaction, then a loud click emanated from the other side of the door.

Becker jumped and considered making a run for it before managing to pull his nerves together. He was still pretty scared, but now that feeling was mixed with something different: anticipation. He took one last look around the area, this time to make sure that no one could see what he was up to, then grabbed the handle and pulled the door wide open.

"Holy—" but the rest was lost in the roar.

Standing in front of him was the mouth of a blue tunnel, which apparently extended into infinity (as opposed to Illuminating Experiences). The tube itself seemed to crackle with electricity, and the noise inside was deafening. Hands shaking, Becker fumbled through his Orientation packet, but the instructions simply told him, "Put on your Transport Goggles™ and make the Leap!"

"Easier said than done," he said out loud, but at this point Becker was pretty sure that Amy's snowball had hit him in the head much harder than he'd first thought. Soon he'd be waking up on the ground with her and a few concerned neighbors asking, "Are you okay?" and then he'd tell them about this crazy dream he'd had when he was out cold. So he figured what the heck, there's nothing to lose—and did what the packet suggested.

He jumped.

The In-Between

The voyage through the vast expanse of electromagnetic blue known as the In-Between has best been described as a combination of "being shot out of a cannon, sky diving, and getting turned inside out," which is why the experienced commuter never eats a thing up to an hour before making the trip. Unfortunately for Becker Drane, it had only been twenty minutes since that bacon, egg, and cheese.

By the time he hit the first turn of the Transport Tube, Becker was blowing chunks all over his brand-new North Face parka. His knapsack had emptied itself midway through the Big Bend, and not even Carmen (the best barber in HP) could rescue what was happening to his hair. But even though Becker felt like his face was about to peel off from the sheer speed, he couldn't suppress a "WHOOOOOOAA!!!!" at what was transpiring all around him.

Everywhere he looked were transparent blue tubes much like the one he was traveling through, only what was moving through those wasn't people. It was packaged goods instead—crates, bags, even canvases rolled up like rugs—all stacked on giant palettes and stamped with the insignia of The Seems. What was inside the containers was impossible to say (for each item was sealed up tightly), but they were all meticulously arranged and headed in the opposite direction.

At this point in the game, Becker's grip on reality (and thus his sanity) had begun to slip. There wasn't much time to worry about it, though, because up ahead a small dot of white was quickly getting closer. It grew bigger and bigger and bigger until everything else in his field of vision was gone save the whiteness itself. There was a burst of cold air, a loud clap, and then . . .

WHAM!

Whatever force had been propelling Becker was gone, and he suddenly found himself on his hands and knees on some kind of soft rubber padding—but he was not alone. A loud burst of applause shot through the air and before he knew it, somebody was giving him a blanket, someone else was shaking his hand and patting him on the back, and still others were telling him how proud they were, what a great moment this was, that they were so glad he had come.

To be honest, all of it was kind of a blur, except the one unforgettable image of a tall black man, with blue-tinted sunglasses and a welcoming grin on his face. Becker figured he must have been somebody important, because the crowd parted as he approached and put a hand upon the boy's shoulder.

"Well done, Mr. Drane," the man said in a thick African accent. "I knew you would make it."

But before Becker could respond, he totally passed out.

Of the sixty-one persons who'd been tapped by Nick Dejanus, five threw out the packet without ever opening it, eight woke up the next morning with cold feet, ten turned back at the sight of the Door, and fifteen opened the Door but couldn't bring themselves to walk through it.[4] That left twenty-three brave souls who'd placed the strange pair of goggles that had been included with the package over their eyes and summoned up the courage to make the Leap.

"The first thing I want to say to each and every one of you is, '*Ìkíniàríyöìkí ayö fún àlejò* Seems,' which in my native language of Yoruba means 'Welcome to The Seems!'"

The same imposing figure who greeted Becker on the Landing Pad now stood in front of a lecture hall, still wearing his blue shades, along with a sweatsuit bearing the initials: "IFR." On the one hand he looked chiseled out of hard obsidian, but on the other, his voice and manner betrayed a deep warmth of spirit.

"I know what many of you must be going through. To find out The World is not what you thought it was can be a very disconcerting thing."

The group of attendees quickly nodded in agreement. They were a motley collection from every corner of the globe, most of whom still looked white as ghosts from the shock of the journey they had just endured.

---

4. This was part of the process of narrowing down the field, and a hefty job for The Cleanup Crew—a division of Human Resources responsible for "humanely unremembering people" of what they knew about The Seems and collecting all hard materials that might leave a paper trail.

"My name is Fixer Jelani Blaque and I will be your guide this day—and hopefully your Instructor for the length of your Training."

A woman in her mid-forties who had spent the last half hour puking her guts out raised her hand and spoke in German.

"Entschuldigen Sie mich, geehrter Herr, aber Training für, was?"

"Aktivieren Sprecheneinfaches™ *Sie bitte Ihr, Frau Von Schroëder,"* suggested Fixer Blaque. Frau Von Schroëder affixed a small plastic tip to her tongue and began to speak in a language that everyone could understand.

"I'm sorry, but I was just wondering where we are exactly?"

"Yeah, yo," spoke up a med student from south-central LA. "Somebody better tell me what's going on up in this joint!"

From the sound of the grumbles, the rest of the crowd seconded this emotion, but Fixer Blaque had been expecting this. He simply smiled and leaned forward on the podium.

"Kevin, kill the lights!"

The lights dimmed and a flat-screen monitor slowly descended from the ceiling. It took a moment or two for the projector to warm up before an image of The World appeared—pristine and shining in green, brown, and blue.

"On the other side of The World, through the Fabric of Reality and across the In-Between, is a place we call The Seems."

Onscreen, an animation kicked in, mirroring the voyage they'd all just taken and ending with a sweeping overhead shot of what looked like a massive corporate complex.

"Here in The Seems, it is our job to build the World you live in from Scratch. From the Department of Weather . . ."

The campus was replaced by images of Weathermen throwing the switches that control the Rain and Snow.

"To the Department of Energy . . ."

A huge magnet was being positioned to ensure that Gravity kept its hold.

"To the Department of Time . . ."

Brass gears were being oiled and cranked by hand.

"Everyone does their best to make The World the most amazing place it can be."

The image shifted to a conference-room table, where a group of high-level executives pored over complex flow charts and graphs.

"As you can imagine, this is quite an extensive operation, and usually things run exactly according to Plan. But sometimes things go wrong, big things that the people in various departments can't handle on their own."

The screen changed to a picture of the sky, which was falling, and a team of ordinary workers who were unable to hold it up.

"And that's when they call in one of us."

Up came an exterior shot of the building they were in right now, which was newer and more modern looking than the rest.

"Here at the IFR, Candidates are given a mastery of the very inner workings of The World and trained to repair the machines that generate Reality itself."

And last but not least, the telltale symbol of a double-sided wrench materialized.

"And though you may not know it yet, each of you contains something within you that has called you to be at this place, at this moment in Time. It will be my job to take that spark and shape it into what we here call . . . a Fixer."

As the lights came up and the Instructor shuffled through his papers, the dazed Candidates sized each other up. There was a shepherd from Kashmir, a computer scientist from New Zealand, a mechanic from Azerbaijan, and even a nine-year-old boy from Highland Park, New Jersey—who had thankfully been revived and given a new set of clothes.

"Tu t'appelle quoi?"

Someone elbowed Becker from the seat next to him.

"Huh?"

It was a cool-looking French teenager in a suede jacket and bandanna. He motioned an apology and attached his own Sprecheneinfaches.

"What's your name, dude?"

"Oh. Becker . . ." Becker slid the translation device over his tongue as well. "Becker Drane."

"Thibadeau Freck."

They shook hands, and immediately Becker felt a whole lot more comfortable. Everybody else in the audience was like "What's this little boy doing here?" but Thibadeau looked at him like there was no question he belonged.

"Pretty trippy, huh?"

"Tell me about it."

Fixer Blaque cleared his throat and called everybody back to attention.

"Now please leave your belongings on your chairs. There is a lot I have to show you."

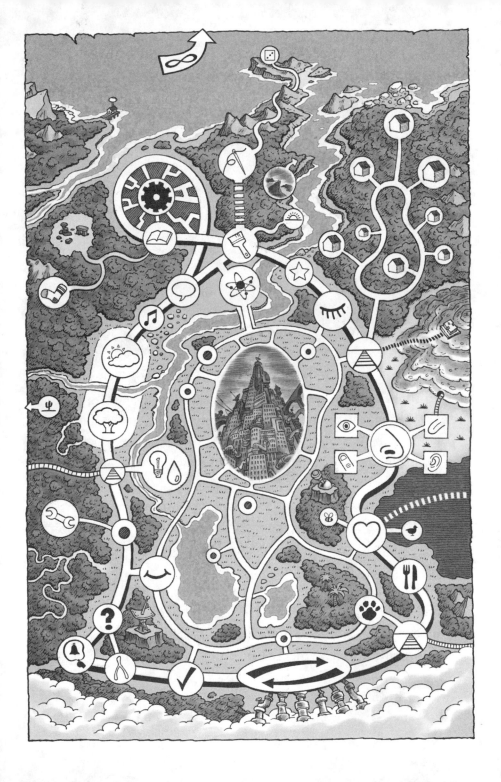

When the tour was over, the Instructor gathered the shell-shocked Candidates on the Field of Play—a huge green expanse at the center of the complex—and shared with them a few parting thoughts. First and foremost, he explained that most of the people who worked in The Seems were born there. But being from The World made one uniquely qualified for the particular job of Fixer, which is why Human Resources only recruited from the other side.

"Which side is the other side?" asked a weird guy with a Sherlock Holmes hat and pipe.

"Whichever side you're not on," quipped Fixer Blaque.

"Oh."

Becker leaned back in the cool grass and took in the sights. Employees on lunch break were throwing disc and a family unpacked cherries from their picnic basket. As far as Becker could tell, The Seems itself wasn't all that different from The World—it's just that the greens were greener and the blues were bluer, and the smell of fresh air was just a little bit fresher. His head was exploding with questions, the first of which was, "Why do they call it The Seems?"—but that's Another Story.[5]

"I was exactly like you once," said the Instructor, adjusting his shades to refract the glare. "Going about my life, trying to survive in what seemed to be a crazy World, yet deep down, always yearning for something . . . more."

The Candidates nodded in recognition. Whatever that something more was, Jelani Blaque seemed to have found it, for there was an "okayness" about him that each and every one of them yearned to have themselves.

---

5. See Appendix B: "Another Story."

"Then one day, in the heat of the lunch-hour sun, I wandered into the marketplace in Abuja, and tucked inside an empty stall—between the bookseller and the juju man—what did I discover?"

"A box with a sign on the front?" asked a Swedish line cook named Jonas Larsson.

"Fisí lòbèrè sàn Jùlô ijë Kékeré Ayéaráyé," replied Blaque. Everybody laughed, remembering the stories of how each of them had found their own box, their own stack of applications and No. 2 pencils. "And let me tell you, friends, 'The Best Job in The World' does not begin to do it justice."

Just then, a blimp passed overhead, loaded with Stars for a new constellation—which only hammered home the scope of the opportunity they were being offered.

"Now, I know this will not be an easy decision for any of you, for you no doubt have families and homes and responsibilities in The World. And there is no shame at all should you choose to decline. But should you accept," his eyes burned with the pride and love of his profession, "I promise this will be the greatest adventure of your life."

Blaque waited for someone to speak, for someone to make a move, but the invitees were frozen in silence. The moment of truth had arrived, and no one knew quite what to do with it . . . until a lone hand rose in the air.

"Mr. Freck?"

With his Serengetti eyewear and five o'clock shadow, the teenaged Frenchman was the epitome of Parisian cool. His weather-burned skin spoke of winters at Chamonix and summers hiking the G-5, and he'd clearly heard all he needed to today.

"Count me in, Monsieur Blaque."

"I already did." The Fixer smiled.

A buzz rippled through the crowd—especially when the youngest member of the group promptly followed suit.

"Count me in too."

Thibadeau extended a fist, Becker bumped it, and the rest—as they say—is History.

When Duty Calls

Lafayette Middle School, Highland Park,
New Jersey—Now

It was a pleasant day in The World, and why not? Fall had settled in and the leaves were that mix of yellow, red, and Occasional Orange they only use one week a year. Over by Lafayette
Middle School, the grounds were eerily silent, for it was only
3:04 p.m. Sixteen minutes later, the bell would ring and the
doors would fly open, and giant backpacks strapped to kids
would streak across the lawns, heading for the yellow school
buses, silver SUVs, or locked-up bicycles that would transport
them into the rest of the day.

In Classroom 6G, Dr. Louis Kole continued his lecture in
Honors English class. "And so, to conclude, though the use of
flashback in *I Am the Cheese* risks alienating the reader, it con-
tributes greatly to the immersive nature of the story world and
is essential to the development of plot."

I Am the Cheese was this week's selection in Dr. Kole's "Best Books Ever" class, but despite the quality of the novel in question, the class had been allotted an eighth-period time slot, which doomed it to a form of mass distraction.

In the back of the classroom, Eva Katz was carving Bobby Miller's name into her desk, while John Webster was staring at a point in the universe that only he could see. But in Aisle 4, Seat #3, another activity was underway. A twelve-year-old boy with shaggy hair and faded corduroys was incessantly checking the black device that was clipped on to his belt.

"Mr. Drane!"

Becker was caught red-handed.

"Perhaps *you* would like to enlighten us on the development of plot?"

He scanned the entire classroom, but finding no aid, was forced to hazard a guess.

"Um . . . it thickens?"

This got a laugh from the peanut gallery, but not the kind you want.

"This is unacceptable!" Dr. Kole was fuming because Becker had always been an honors student, but lately his GPA had begun to suffer. "If you want to be a space cadet, English B is down the hall."

"Sorry, Doc." Becker truly meant it—he knew his teacher loved literature, and he didn't want to disappoint him. "I've just got a lot on my mind these days."

"I can see that. Maybe a few sessions with Mrs. Horner will help clear that up."

Mrs. Horner was the vice-principal in charge of discipline

and no one wanted a piece of that. Thankfully, Becker was saved by the proverbial bell.

"Remember, young readers—pop quiz tomorrow!"

Amid the stampede for the door, Jeremy Mintz couldn't resist—

"Then it's not pop!"

"NO INCOMING CALLS."

Becker's Blinker™ flashed the same disappointing message it had moments earlier, so he clipped it back on his belt, got on his bike, and began the short trip home.

Highland Park was (and always had been) Becker's hometown, and as the sign on Route 27 declared, it's "A Nice Place to Live." There are crookety sidewalks and tree-lined streets and a nice little main drag with shops and stores and a post office. Becker had spent the last three years bopping back and forth between HP and the IFR and just as Fixer Blaque had promised, Training had been a pretty wild ride. It not only taught him the art of Fixing but literally changed the way he looked at The World. Whereas once it was just a place to hang out and go to school, now all he could see around him were the amazing creations of the various departments. And judging by the way the sky, the clouds, the very sound of the wind through the trees were coming together to create this perfect autumn afternoon, someone was on their game today.

Anyhow, Becker dropped his bike on the front lawn of 12 Grant Avenue and bounded through the wide front door.

"Anybody home?"

"I'm in the kitchen!"

Samantha Mitchell was one of the most sought-after babysitters in town, because a) she gave the kids a pretty long leash, and b) she was one of the prettiest girls at HPHS. Currently, she was locked in a conference call regarding invites to her Sweet Sixteen.

"Where's Benjamin?"

"Up in the playroom."

Becker trundled up the stairs, barging in on his brother, who sat guiltily in front of the third-floor TV. Ben was six to Becker's twelve, but that didn't stop him from indulging in another round of *Juvenile Delinquent*.

"Dude, I just toilet-papered the Senior Center!"

In the bestselling video game, it was your mission to vandalize as much of an unsuspecting town as possible before getting busted by parents, teachers, or the local 5-0. They had gotten a bootlegged copy from Kyle Fox, the infamous black-marketeer of M-rated vids, and though it was far from appropriate for a child of Benjamin's age, that's what afternoons with the babysitter were all about.

"Put it on two-player!" Becker picked up a controller and quickly entered the fray. "Faster, B, he's right on your tail."

A heavy-set truant officer was chasing Benjamin down a back alley.

"I'm trying!"

Becker pressed the "A" button and "Quentin"—the sketchy burnout he'd created as his alter ego—suddenly popped from behind a garbage can and emptied a case of thumbtacks onto the concrete. While the hapless officer fell to the ground in agony, a message onscreen flashed "10,000 Bonus Points," and the brothers made their hasty escape.

"Thanks, dude." Benjamin breathed a sigh of relief.

"No sweat."

They high-fived each other (onscreen and off-), then Quentin fired up his motorized scooter.

"Now let's go egg City Hall!"

Wednesday nights were movie night, when Benjamin went to bed early and Becker got to log some QT with Samantha Mitchell. Though Samantha was four years Becker's senior (and dating Tommy Vanderlin[6]), he was working his deep-cover strategy of convincing her that even though the age difference between them now seemed insurmountable, it wouldn't always be that way.

"Pass me the popcorn, would you?" asked Samantha, reaching across the cushiony L-shaped couch.

Becker handed it over, then casually took another peek at the Blinker on his belt.

"STILL NO INCOMING CALLS."

Bummer. It had been five long weeks since Becker had received his promotion to Fixer, but he still hadn't gotten a call. A regular working Fixer gets about one Mission every two to three weeks, which is about how long it takes for the Rotation to turn over, and Fixer #36 (aka "No-Hands Phil") had been called in to lift a Cloud of Suspicion over ten days ago. That meant Fixer #37 (aka Becker Drane) was next up on the list, and he was chomping at the bit to get his first Mission.

---

6. Quarterback of the Highland Park Owls football team (currently 0–6).

"This is a really good flick," interrupted his babysitter. Becker shook off his preoccupation with The Seems and returned to his living room couch.

"Cool. I thought you might like it."

Tonight, Becker had selected *The Real Thing* for their viewing entertainment, an obscure indie feature about a young girl who struggles to find love, until the quirky yet strangely perfect man of her dreams sweeps her off her—

"I can't sleep!"

Benjamin appeared on the landing with his blankie in hand.

"Well, go back up and try again!" Becker was motioning to him like "get lost, you're blowing my rap," but Benjamin was oblivious. (Or at least pretending to be.)

"Becker, go upstairs and help your little brother."

Becker dropped his head, defeated—then jumped off the couch and chased the little mongrel up the stairs.

"You better hope I don't catch you!"

Though the Drane house was fairly well kempt, the two brothers had worn a path on the wool carpeting that lined the stairways and halls. One set of feet was small (but quick), while the other was big (but even quicker), which lent Becker a decided advantage in the race.

"Don't hit me! I'm gonna tell Mom!" screeched Benjamin, as he tucked and rolled into his room.

"Not if you're already dead!"

Even Becker had to admit his brother's bedroom was the sweetest in the house. Benjamin had gone through about a hundred phases already in his short life and all the residual evidence from those periods was scattered about hither-nither. He had a race-car bed (from when he wanted to be a race-car driver), glow-in-the-dark planets on the ceiling (from when he wanted to be an astronaut), and a host of giant canvases (because now he was in his "artist phase").

"Back in bed, Benja-bratt." Ben got into the driver's seat, while Becker took up a position on one of the Pirelli tires. "Now, what's your problem?"

"I couldn't sleep. I swear, it's not my fault."

"Then whose fault is it?"

"She's too old for you, anyway."

Becker lunged at his little brother, who ducked under the blankets. But when he came back up for air, he had clearly shifted gears. Gone was the abominable snowchild, and in his place was a charming little bro.

"Will you tell me another story about The Seems?"

Talking to Benjamin about The Seems was semi against the Rules, but Becker had shared select pieces with him because a) he was young and got afraid a lot, and b) even if he ever did say something to someone, they would probably just think he had a great imagination. Which he did.

"What do you wanna know?"

"I want to hear about the Night They Robbed the Memory Bank."

"I already told you that one."

"Then tell me about Ice Cream Sunday."

Becker sighed because he had already told him that one too, but he figured if he got it over quickly, maybe he could get back downstairs in time for the final scene, when tears would flow and he might get a "Becker, that was so sweet," from Samantha Mitchell.

"Every year in The Seems—"

"Tell it like you mean it!"

Becker thought about suggesting to his parents (again) that Benjamin endure a short stint at military school, but that idea had been rejected. Plus, this was one of his favorites too.

"Every year in The Seems, on the most beautiful day imaginable, there's a national holiday that they call Ice Cream Sunday."

"That's better."

"Everyone except for the Skeleton Crew gets the day off, and the entire Field of Play is transformed into a giant festival. There's music and rides, and all the different departments set up these giant tents. The Department of Time hands out Déjà Vu's, Nature has a Cloud Walk, and Public Works auctions off all the best Sunsets of the year. Even the Food & Drink Administration lets you sample all the newest treats before they hit The World."

"Have you ever been to Ice Cream Sunday?"

"Once—as a Briefer, and it was pretty awesome. But now that I'm a Fixer, I get a VIP pass, which lets you in to all the private parties and even gets you backstage at the Jam Session."

"Man, I wanna be a Fixer!"

"I thought you wanted to be a Sunset Painter."

"I wanna be both."

Becker shook his head in amazement. Kids.

"Now go to sleep before Mom comes home and we're both up a creek."

Benjamin nodded and tucked himself in, but it was obvious that something was still bothering him.

"Becker?"

"What?"

"Um . . . if there's The Seems and they have a Plan and stuff . . . then . . . then how come Amy died?"

Ouch. That was something Becker tried not to think about anymore.

About a year ago, his best friend, Amy Lannin, had gone into the hospital for a routine operation, but there had been complications and she never came out. Becker was crushed, and Benjamin too (because she had always protected him from the local bullies), yet he had never brought it up since the day both of them had been pulled out of class to hear the terrible news.

"That's a good question, B."

Becker swallowed the lump in his throat, then found the same answer that someone had given him one night, when he was feeling much the same way.

"No one, not even a Case Worker, can see into the heart of the Plan. And beware of anyone who says that they can." Then he leaned in and whispered in Benjamin's ear. "But here's what I believe—"

"All right, you two!"

Both the boys whirled around to see their mother in the doorway. Her arms were crossed and it was impossible to tell how much of the conversation she had heard.

"Enough Dungeons and Dragons for one night!"

"It's not Dungeons and Dragons. It's The Seems!" Benjamin shook his head in amazement. Adults.

As Mrs. Drane took over the parenting duties, Becker backed out carefully and tried to slip away.

"Where do you think you're going, young man?"

51

"To finish my movie."

"Your movie's finished." Uh-oh. Becker had heard this tone before and it wasn't a good sign. "Go brush your teeth and meet me in your room."

By any reasonable standard, Dr. Natalie Drane was a pretty cool mom. She was a psychologist by trade, which meant she tended to be rather forgiving if some sort of minor transgression should occur. But on the flip side, she liked to have these "talks." There was a talk when Becker "borrowed" a Reese's Peanut Butter Cup from Foodtown (he was only four at the time). And there was a talk about smoking, red meat, the dangers of the Internet, and the importance of sharing, especially when it came to feelings.

"Guess who I got a phone call from today?"

Becker crawled into his bed and prepared to take his lumps.

"I give up."

"Dr. Kole. He says you've been very distracted in class lately and wanted to know if anything was wrong at home."

Well, Becker thought, the snack drawer was rather empty as of late and a sixty-eight-inch flat-screen TV might be a nice addition, but other than that . . .

"You're out the door before breakfast, you lock yourself in your room when you get home, and you're up all hours of the night." She cleared her throat, not relishing what might come next. "Is there something you want to tell me?"

Actually, there was—that he'd gotten promoted to Fixer and the reason he was distracted was far more important than Dr. Kole and his Best Books Ever.

"Yes, but I'm not allowed to."

"Is this about that game again?"

Becker nodded, pretending to be embarrassed. Like every other Fixer, he had developed a cover story, in case someone in his life started to get suspicious. Some Fixers used second jobs or boyfriends/girlfriends, but his idea was that The Seems was just this underground role-playing game that all the kids were into these days, and that seemed to work pretty well.

"Listen, Becks, if you and your brother want to save the world, that's fine. But not if it gets in the way of your studies."

"Fair enough." Becker hated to let his mother down, but when she reached into her pocketbook and pulled out a brand-new copy of *I Am the Cheese*—"Aw c'mon, Mom! That book is way too dark for someone my age. Besides, you'd have to be a rocket scientist to figure it out!"

"Well, luckily you're not a rocket scientist."

Becker had to admit, his mom was pretty good. She kissed him on the forehead, turned out the lights, and issued her usual farewell.

"Now sleep tight, and don't let the bed bugs bite!"

But as soon as she closed the door Becker tossed the book aside, for there was really only one thing on his mind: when was his Mission going to come through? On the one hand, radio silence was a good thing, because that meant all was right in The Seems (and hence The World), but on the other, it was starting to make him nervous. Maybe they had found an error on his Practical and he hadn't been added to the Rotation. Or maybe his Blinker was on the fritz. Or worse yet, maybe someone in the Big Building had woken up in the middle of the night in a cold sweat, and realized, "Wait a minute. I can't put a twelve-year-old in a position as important as this."

With his mind racing, the young Fixer shut his eyes and tried to remember all the tricks he'd learned over the past three years. Don't stress out over what you can't control. Trust your Case Worker. And rest assured that everything happens according to Plan. The more he reminded himself, the more he felt his body starting to relax. The bed felt comfy beneath him. The pillows were soft and cool. And with a hearty yawn, he pulled the blanket tight and strapped himself in for another good night's sleep.

Two hours later, Becker sat up in his bed, mildly disturbed. On most nights he had little trouble sleeping and it usually only took a moment or two before he felt that pleasant feeling of "sliding across." But for some reason, on this night it didn't go that way. Every time he felt himself beginning to slide, he would invariably get bounced back. It was almost like someone had put up an invisible wall, a barrier to sleep that could not be surmounted no matter how hard he tried. Becker rolled over, changed pillows, repositioned his legs, even counted sheep, but nothing seemed to work.

Without warning, a light in the hallway flicked on and two small feet went chugging past his door. From the sound of sirens wailing, his little brother was back at "Juvee" again, yet this was of little concern. Benjamin often had trouble getting his Z's. It was only when he heard his mom and dad's voices chatting through the wall that his 7th Sense began to flare.

A lot of people talk about the 6th Sense—that it's ESP or talking to dead people, but those are actually your 10th and 11th

Senses. The 6th Sense is in fact your sense of humor and the 8th Sense is your sense of direction (both doled out in varying quantities), but the 7th Sense is an entirely different animal.[7] That's a feeling you get when something has gone wrong in The Seems and will soon affect The World. Few ever learn to cultivate it, but properly honed it is one of the Fixer's greatest assets, for the sensations can lead you straight to the source of the problem. Becker Drane was one of those few, and when he felt the hairs on his neck beginning to rise, he got out of the bed.

From his second-story window there was a view of Highland Park, and he could see the Dranes were not alone in their affliction. Mrs. Chudnick lived next door and she was standing in her kitchen, warming up some milk. The Croziers were across the street, playing their own games of solitaire in each of their bedrooms. And Paul the Wanderer, who lived in his car (he was harmless so the cops let it slide) was reading *War and Peace* by the dashboard light. In fact, all across the neighborhood lights were on and people were wide awake.

For Becker to be up at this hour was plausible—he was leading a dual life with double responsibilities and homework in two worlds—but the rest of these people were just ordinary citizens who were usually fast asleep by now. The feeling on the back of Becker's neck made its way to his stomach and would soon be causing a prickly set of chills all over. This was the progression of the 7th Sense and it could only mean one thing: something had gone wrong in The Seems.

Something big.

---

7. Note: The 9th Sense is not so easily explained, but it has a lot to do with interior design.

Gandan Monastery, Sühbaatar Province, Outer Mongolia

Precisely thirty-three seconds earlier, the inimitable Li Po's eyes opened upon the sacred temple that he called home. He'd been contemplating The Most Amazing Thing of All when his own neck hairs had raised, and now he waited serenely for Central Command to send out its Call.

"OMMMMMM."

As the chanting of the monks reverberated through the chamber, Fixer #1 on the Rotation wiped the sweat from his brow. He was the acknowledged master of the 7th Sense, and whatever was happening in The Seems during the eternal moment of Now, he was the first to feel it. But tonight, he couldn't get a lock on which Department had gone down.

Perhaps it was Weather again. Or Time. Or maybe even . . .

Gordon's Bay Retirement Community, Cape Town, South Africa

Nature. It had to be Nature. She had sent a memo about a patch of purple grass in Senegal, but the Big Building had ignored her, and now look what was happening.

"Sylvia! It's your move!"

It took the Fixer known as "The Octogenarian" a moment to remember where she was and what she was doing there. Oh, yes. This was the final round of the annual GB Canasta Championship, and a crowd of onlookers anxiously waited to see if she and Morty could defend their title.

"Gotta run, darlings!" Sylvia smiled and threw down the final meld for a clean knockout. "Time for my morning massage."

Leaving her opponents (and the fans) in a state of shock, Fixer #3 adjourned to the Clubhouse and pulled a little black box from her oversized pocketbook. In her fifty years on the Duty Roster, Sylvia Nichols had seen all there was to see, but the thrill of another Mission about to go out never got old. She quickly toggled over to every Fixer's favorite Blinker screen:

"MISSION IN PROGRESS."

So did Tony the Plumber, Mr. Chiappa, Anna-Julia Rafaella Carolina dos Santos, and thirty other Fixers around The World (and hopefully Tom Jackal), all of whom at this exact moment had stepped away from their dinner party or baccarat table or teachers' convention or walk on the beach or lifelong search for an ancient artifact to see what exactly had gone wrong, and what kind of job they were going to give the kid.

But one Fixer found out first.

12 Grant Avenue, Highland Park, New Jersey

BLINK! BLINK! BLINK! BLINK! BLINK!

In the middle of his sweaty palm, Becker's Blinker was flashing off the hook. He couldn't believe it was actually happening. And it was actually happening now!

"Time to make the doughnuts."

With a deep breath, he pressed the yellow "accept" button

and the box began to transform. A miniature-sized keyboard extended from the base and the view-screen expanded to twice its usual size. Audio came in first—a high whine settling to a low hum—followed by a fuzzy image, which gradually faded into view.

A double-sided wrench.

"Stand by for transmission."

Becker jacked in his headphones and locked his door as the Fixer logo was quickly replaced by a chiseled face with piercing blue eyes.

"Fixer 37, F. Becker Drane. Please report. Over!"

The Dispatcher wore a headset and uniform, and his buzz-cut was perfectly manicured. But he rarely engaged in small talk.

"37, present and accounted for!"

"Prepare for Verification."

A handprint appeared on the screen and Becker matched his palm to it. Light rolled over his lifeline and a computerized voice began to speak.

"Verification complete. Prepare for Personality Scan."

Almost everything else about a person can be replicated, except for his or her personality. A thin beam quickly examined Becker's interior world.

"Personality confirmed!"

The important part came next.

"Mission Report: Seems-World Time 24:27."

Becker pulled out his pad and waited for the details.

"Glitch reported—Department of Sleep. Assignment: Find and Fix!"

His pen froze inches above the paper.

"Excuse me, sir, but did you say Glitch?"

"Say again: Glitch reported—Department of Sleep. Assignment: Find and Fix!"

Becker was in a state of shock. A glitch in The World was just a common mechanical breakdown, but a Glitch in The Seems was a rare and serious threat. In fact, there hadn't been a confirmed Glitch in any department since the Day That Time Stood Still,[8] and the Fixer who went on that Mission—

"Do we have Mission confirmation?"

The sound of the Dispatcher's voice snapped him back into the present.

"Mission accepted and confirmed!"

"Your Briefer will meet you when you get to Sleep. Oh, and kid . . ." the corner of his mouth might've just turned up a little, *"welcome to the big leagues."*

And just like that, the signal went out, the screen folded down, and Becker was left alone in the darkness of his room.

---

8. November 5, 1997.

The Mission Inside the Mission

"Move, Becker. Move."

Back in his bedroom, precious seconds were ticking away, but Becker couldn't bring himself to take a step.

"What's wrong with you, dude?"

The simple fact of the matter was that he was terrified. Why couldn't he have just gotten a Foible or a Broken Window like Fixer #35? The Rotation was random in that way—no matter what the Mission was (except under the "Special Circumstances" clause that was used very infrequently), whoever was up next got whatever came up next. But never in his wildest dreams did he imagine he would have to take on a Glitch.

"Pull it together, Candidate Drane!" Thankfully, a familiar voice started booming in his head. *"Never be afraid to be afraid!"*

Jelani Blaque was one of the greatest Fixers who ever lived, and Becker's Training under him had been so rigorous that it sometimes felt as if his Instructor was still right there, over his shoulder, shouting out encouragement.

"Remember your ìwà, *for there is wisdom in the repetition!"*

"Remember my *ìwà*," Becker closed his eyes. "Remember my *ìwà*."

Ìwà was Yoruba for "practice," which Blaque demanded constantly of his Candidates. Every day at the beginning of Training, they would practice their Procedures, and though it sometimes got tedious, the benefits of this technique were now becoming clear.

"Take out your Toolkit and commence equipment check!"

The newest and youngest of the Fixers finally got his right foot to take a step . . . then his left . . . then reached down under his bed to remove his brand-new Toolkit. It was a Toolmaster 3000™, the latest in the messenger-bag style, complete with deluxe Tools, reinforced pockets, and plenty of extra Space.[9] He opened the flap to confirm that everything he needed for the Mission was ready and waiting.

"Then deploy your Me-2™!"

In Becker's humble opinion, the Me-2 was one of the cleverest Tools to ever come out of the Shed. It looked like an inflatable life vest, but when he pulled the two red tabs, it blew up to become a life-sized replica of . . . himself! On the back was a dial with various settings—"At Work," "At Play," "Auto-Pilot"—and Becker set his to "Asleep" and placed it in his bed. Instantly it began to breathe in and out with a slight, well-executed snore.

"Next, implement your exit strategy!"

---

9. Toolmaster 3000s are bigger on the inside than on the out.

When he had been stuck at the beach for Labor Day, Becker had busted out his Me-2 underwater and made a swim for it. And when he couldn't escape from Rachel Adler's bat mitzvah that day, he'd been forced to slip away during the height of the limbo contest and slide out through the kitchen door. But tonight he just had to make sure that his mom and dad and Benjamin didn't hear him crawl out the second-story window, climb down the branches of the backyard elm tree, and fire up his Trek hybrid.

"And last but not least, prepare to make the Leap!"

As Becker pedaled feverishly down Harrison Avenue and back toward Cleveland, the malady that afflicted The World was obvious in every house along the way. TVs were flickering at desperate families. Board games were being removed from shelves. Even Dr. Kole was busy in his duplex on North Second, putting the finishing touches on tomorrow's killer quiz. It was times like this that Becker wished the Skeleton Key proposal had been ratified in The Seems. That initiative had called for an abandonment of the old Door system—in which portals were scattered throughout The World, often in plain sight— and the issuing of special keys that could open a seam anywhere in the Fabric of Reality. This would have been especially useful for Fixers and Briefers (who needed to get across at a moment's notice), but the referendum was summarily shot down by those resistant to change and a coalition of the Unwilling.

Becker cruised to a halt at the back of Illuminating Experiences, and though he had made the Leap over a hundred times by now, this time felt very much like the first. He waited for a late-night jogger to pass by, her fluorescent vest glinting under a single streetlight, then quietly made his way through the leaves and back to the landing of the stairs.

Someone had recently painted graffiti over the symbol on the door and, given the praises to Black Sabbath and Satan, Becker chalked it up to his friend Leo, a *real* juvenile delinquent, but with a heart of gold. Becker laughed and this helped him relax a little bit, but as he reached forward and swiped his brand-new laminate, Becker couldn't get rid of the dryness in his mouth.

"Now there's one last thing, Candidate . . ."

Fortunately, Fixer Blaque's voice was still ringing in his ears.

"When in doubt, always remember . . . The World is counting on you!"

Becker pulled down his Transport Goggles and yanked the door ajar. Blue light spilled over his face and the highways and byways of the In-Between lay sprawled out before him.

"And so am I!"

Customs, Department of Transportation, The Seems

When Becker arrived at the Landing Pad, his Transport Goggles were covered in frost. Though the trip through the In-Between was gnarly, it also had its perks. If you kept your head about you (and didn't smash into anything), you could get a great preview of what was heading for The World that day— Shooting Stars, Twists of Fate, Big Ideas—all prepackaged and ready to be enjoyed.

"Laminate and purpose for your visit?"

Becker flashed his Badge, and the Customs Official flinched, knowing that if a Fixer was in attendance, something big must be afoot.

"This way, sir!"

The Terminal was bustling, packed with Quality Control, Agents of L.U.C.K., and tourists on their way back from The World.[10] Though they were all waiting on the typically long de-briefing line, no one seemed annoyed that Becker was sliding by them via "Express." That's because they had all been in The World when the Glitch hit and were keenly aware of its drastic effects.

". . . it's about time."

". . . hasn't been a Glitch since . . ."

". . . a bit young to be a Fixer?"

The idle chatter didn't help Becker's confidence, so he tuned it out because he had a job to do. He quickly made his way through the crowd and boarded the first monorail that stopped at the Department of Sleep.

"Now arriving, Department of Love! Please stand clear of the clos-ing doors!"

Becker held on to the pole as the train started up again and continued on its loop around The Seems. Because of the late hour, most of the passengers were already on their commute home, but Becker's day had just begun.

---

10. Every employee in The Seems gets two weeks of paid vacation, and The World is a perennial hot spot.

"Now arriving, the Olfactory! Please apply nose plugs and stand clear of the closing doors!"

"As if nose plugs would stop that smell . . ."

A rider next to him was gripping one of the hanging straps, eyes red and drooping from a long day on the job.

"How'd it go today?" asked Becker.

"Basic Reality Check, hit the W and make sure green is green, red is red, E still equals MC^2."

"That must be an awesome job."

"Ahh, 'nother day, 'nother dollar. How 'bout you?"

Becker thought about telling him about his Mission, but he didn't want to bum him out at the end of his shift.

"Same ol', same ol'. World needs its goods and services."

"They got it good over there, don't they?"

"Tell me about it."

"Now arriving, the Jitney! Transfer for service to Here, There, Everywhere, Alphabet City, and Crestview.[11] *Please stand clear of the closing doors!"*

"Catch you on the Flip Side," said the Reality Checker, as he headed home for the evening.

"On the Flip Side."

Becker peered out the window, trying to stop his hands from shaking. The Big Building was all lit up at the center of the loop, and he couldn't help but wonder what was being planned that very moment. For the sake of his Mission, he hoped it was something good.

"Now arriving, Department of Sleep! Please keep your voice down and stand clear of the closing doors!"

---

11. A gated community overlooking the Sunset Strip.

"Simly Alomonus Frye, Briefer #356, reporting for duty, sir!"

Before Becker had even stepped onto the platform, a tall, lanky Seemsian in his mid-twenties was standing at full salute.[12]

"At ease, Simly," said Becker to his Briefer. "I know who you are."

The two had been at the IFR together, and though they hung out in different circles, everyone knew Simly Frye. While most Candidates spent their off time chilling in the Game Room or on the Nature Trail, Simly was a staple at the Library, constantly studying up on some arcane Tool or following a poor Instructor around the halls, begging for details about this Mission or that. Truth be told, you might not want to hang out with him on a Saturday night, but you couldn't ask for a more capable Briefer.

"What on earth are you wearing, dude?"

Becker wasn't referring to Simly's Coke-bottle glasses—which made his eyes look like a bug's—but to the assortments of gadgets, devices, and other random tchotchkes that were strapped all over his body.

"The latest in Fixer technology, sir. And a few classics from back in the Day. For example, check out this—"

Becker stopped him before he could start.

"Forget I asked."

They hopped on the escalator and began ramping up to Sleep.

---

12. For full description of all differences (anatomical and otherwise) between Seemsians and Humans, please see: *The Same, but Different,* by Sitriol B. Flook (copyright XVCGIIYT, Seemsbury Press).

"Can you believe this, sir? You and me? A Glitch?" Simly was a bundle of nerves. "There hasn't been a Glitch in The Seems since the Day That Time Stood Still and the Fixer who—"

"I know what happened."

"Yes, sir. Of course you do."

At the top of the escalator was a sprawling factory, with an elegant courtyard situated out front. Trees and benches were laid out geometrically, giant Night Lights cast a gentle glow, and in the middle, a granite sculpture celebrated the Department of Sleep's famed insignia: a single closed eye.

"Cool. I've never been to this department before," admitted Simly.

"I've only been here a couple of times myself," seconded Becker, "but those were on Field Trips—never on a Mission."

They stopped to read a quotation that was engraved beneath the sculpted eye:

> Now, blessings light on him that first invented sleep! It covers a man all over, thoughts and all, like a cloak; it is meat for the hungry, drink for the thirsty, heat for the cold, and cold for the hot. It is the current coin that purchases all the pleasures of the world cheap, and the balance that sets the king and the shepherd, the fool and the wise man, even.
>
> —*Miguel de Cervantes, 1605 W.T.*[14]

"Who's that guy?" asked Simly, far more versed in Seemsian literature than that of The World.

---

14. W.T.: World Time.

"He's this dude from Spain who wrote a book called *Don Quixote*. I read it in my Best Books Ever class. Well, at least I read the *Cliff's Notes*."

Simly was impressed.

Becker radioed in. "Drane to Central Command, come in, over?"

His orange Receiver was back in working order, the short circuits repaired from the Portuguese rainstorm.

"We read you, Fixer Drane."

"I have Briefer acquisition and we are ready to proceed."

"Understood. Permission granted to enter department."

Almost immediately a silent alarm sounded, and the industrial-sized doors to Sleep began to slide apart.

Central Shipping, Department of Sleep, The Seems

"Thank the Plan you're here!"

From the observation deck above, a small man in a Department of Sleep hard hat came trundling down the stairs. He was the Foreman of Central Shipping, and he'd been anxiously waiting for them.

"A Glitch in Sleep! I can't believe this is happening!"

The middle manager was beside himself, so Becker took a page from Casey Lake and stayed on an even keel.

"Just relax and tell me what went wrong."

"The system was running like clockwork, until we noticed a Blip," recounted the Foreman. "At first we thought it was just a blown Exhaustion Pipe, but then the Insomnia spread like wildfire, and the next thing we knew, we had a Sleepless Night on our hands!"

The Foreman looked both ways to make sure that no one else was listening, then leaned in to Becker's ear.

"Do you think it could be The Tide?"

Becker put a finger to his lips, because he didn't want to foster rumor and innuendo. The Tide was a shadowy organization bent on overthrowing the Powers That Be and assuming control of The World. For the last few months its attacks had increased, both in scope and in frequency, culminating with the assault on the Rain Tower during Becker's final Mission as a Briefer. But whether it were involved in this was still too early to tell.

"Don't worry," Becker reassured him. "That's what we're here to find out."

As the Foreman led them across the factory floor, Simly pulled out his Briefing and began to take notes on Central Shipping. The components of Sleep proper were manufactured in other parts of the department, then carried here via a complex latticework of conveyor belts, tubes, hooks, and ramps before finally being stuffed into little brown boxes, each with its own destination address.

Jami Marmor
Sector 302
MALLEGBERG HOTEL, Room 204

David Bauer
Sector 12
Nir Etzion Kibbutz
Third Cabin, Top Bunk, White Sleeping Bag

Ariff Ng
Sector 904
Carroll 16B, Desk #5
University Of Malaysia

Each box was completely unique and designed for a specific individual, which explains why on some nights you get a little Sleep and on some nights you get a lot. Once they were packed, the boxes were sealed and twined, stamped *"Good Night's Sleep"* by Inspector #9, then they began their final journey down and out an exit hatch, through the In-Between, and ultimately to each and every recipient in The World.

Tonight, however, the exit hatch was shut tight. Boxes of Good Night's Sleep were bunching up at the door, and Tireless Workers raced to gather them before they hit the floor. Alarms were sounding and panic was in the air.

Night Watchmen's Station, Department of Sleep, The Seems

"It's more serious than we thought." Night Watchman #1 adjusted his headset and toggled through his Cases. "And it's only getting worse."

Becker and Simly crowded closer to the Night Watchmen's flat-panel Window. It was his (and his staff's) task to watch over the sleepers of The World, and make sure everything went according to Plan. Which, unfortunately, it was not.

"Check this one out."

Down on his LCD monitor, a married couple in Greenland

were tossing and turning in their bed. Apparently, their inability to Sleep had provoked a nasty fight, complete with thrown plates and comments they would soon regret.

"Was this expected to happen?" inquired Becker.

"Negative. Totally uncalled for." Night Watchman #1 took another sip of his day-old coffee. "And take a look at Sector 4."

An old man in Katmandu was juggling in bed, while two identical twins were busy playing patty-cake.

"Or Sector 12 . . ."

In Irktusk, Russia, an ice-fisherman was desperately trying to catch those last few Z's before heading back onto the lake, but with absolutely no luck at all.

"Pull up Sector 33, Grid 514." Becker threw in his own request, and the Watchman focused in on Highland Park. Everyone from his hometown was there: Dr. Kole, Mrs. Chudnick, Paul the Wanderer. And at 12 Grant Avenue, Becker's mom and dad and Benjamin were all still wide awake.

"Other than *you*," the Night Watchman flipped to Becker's room, where his Me-2 was snoring happily away, "no one in the entire World is even getting a wink."

Suddenly, another alarm split the air. And this one sounded like trouble.

"I've got a Chain of Events slippage!"

"What?" Becker and Simly gazed upward to see another row of Night Watchmen. And another row above them. "What Sector?"

"1904!"

Night Watchman #1 flipped to Sector 1904 and there was a man in a small motel desperately trying to get some rest.

"Uh-oh."

"What is it?"

"That salesman has been on the road for two weeks and he's trying to make it home for his daughter's birthday. But if he doesn't get some Sleep tonight, he might pass out at the wheel!"

"I've got a Slippage in 906!"

In this Sector, a lonely woman in Istanbul was supposed to get a nap so she would wake up just in time to feel a gentle breeze with the scent of jasmine on it, which might cause her to walk outside and bump into the humble postman who had always wondered if he would ever find his one true love. But if she couldn't get to Sleep, that whole ball of yarn would come undone.

"Slippage in 1743!"

"Another one?"

Becker was starting to get concerned, for Chains of Events were a tricky and complex business. They were put together by Case Workers in the Big Building, sometimes after years of thinking and strategizing, and then locked into the Plan via rubber cement. If you ever saw one in person it would look like a double helix, complete with interlocking pieces and small white tags attached to each event, describing its focus, purpose, and level of importance. But—and this is a big but—if they began to come apart, one could affect the other, and so on and so forth (for all events are interconnected). And if enough Chains were compromised, then the unthinkable could take place.

"Ripple Effect," said Becker, and just the mention of the words cast a pall into the room.

"Plan forbid," said Night Watchman #1. "But if the Glitch

continues unchecked and we can't get Sleep back online, it's a distinct poss—"

"I've got a slippage in 26!"

"No!"

"Slippage in 1804!"

"601!"

"302!"

As the Night Watchmen struggled to manage the crisis, Becker backed away from the Windows, and for the first time that night, he began to feel the magnitude of what was taking place. There were not merely a handful of Night Watchmen, or a dozen, but rather hundreds, perhaps thousands, stacked row upon row on top of each other, rising into the air as far as the eye could see. On every monitor was a Sleepless person. In every chair, a Night Watchman was on the verge of freaking out.

"What are we gonna do, sir?"

Hundreds of pairs of eyes turned to Becker, as if he were the one that could rescue them from this impending nightmare. His mouth felt dry again and his heart began to pound, and for a second he thought he might pass out. But luckily, there was somewhere *he* could turn . . .

Beside the Nature Trail and just off the Beaten Track, there exists a small complex where those in attendance are given Tools (both literal and figurative) with which to save The World. And just as Becker had done when recalling his Procedures, he now harkened back to those halcyon days when he was sculpted into the form and shape of what they call a Fixer.

Mission Simulator "F," Institute for Fixing & Repair— Two and a Half Years Ago

It was a rainy day at the IFR. Droplets fell off the poplar trees and onto the marble statue of Jayson—legendary founder of the Fixers—which was hand-carved with his famous last words: "LIVE TO FIX. FIX TO LIVE."

Every Candidate who walked through these doors lived by that credo, but not all of them could reach that lofty plateau. At this point in the process, Becker's class had dwindled to seventeen (six had dropped out due to injury and one for "personal reasons"), but those who had remained were beaming, because they had finally left the classroom and were getting their first taste of the Mission Simulators.

"It's about time," touted Becker, anxious to see a real Mission in the (virtual) flesh. Thibadeau Freck, the Frenchman he'd met that first day at Orientation, walked beside him, tightening his IFR bandanna.

"What? You're not satisfied learning how to change the air filter on a Stink Tank?"

"Only if I can scrub out the inside of a Fog Horn first."

Becker laughed as they entered the door marked "F." He and the Parisian teenager had become fast friends and would often partner up in Shop or shoot pool in the Game Room during breaks. Thib was anxious to continue their contest of one-upsmanship, when—

"Quiet, Candidates!" Fixer Blaque hushed everyone to attention. "I know everyone's excited, but this is one of the most important lessons you will learn about Fixing, so focus."

Unlike some gurus or teachers whom Becker had run into in his time, Blaque's "lessons" weren't really lessons at all—they were more like really cool vids or tricks of the trade—and Becker often wondered why he wasn't still practicing in the field. Rumor had it that Blaque had been #2 on the Duty Roster and in line to receive the Torch, but something happened to him on a Mission, and he was forced into early retirement.

"Please begin the simulation!"

One of the Mechanics[15] inserted a cartridge labeled "The Day That Time Stood Still" into a clunky-looking player, and the nondescript room was instantly transformed.

"Take it in, people." The Candidates now stood in a holographic reproduction of a vault in the Department of Time. On that fateful day, uniformed workers bearing the insignia of a brass gear were running about in a state of extreme duress. "See what can be seen."

A Time Keeper, rendered in perfect detail, ran directly through Becker's stomach, causing him to reach down and confirm his intestines were still intact.

"Save the Frozen Moments!" The Keeper was carrying a tray of ice cubes, each with a preserved image of something happening inside. "It's a Meltdown! A Meltdown!"

"Now notice Fixer Jackal." Blaque turned the attention of the class to the corner of the room, where an older Fixer in a sheepskin bomber jacket and aviator helmet was struggling to stem the tide of cubes that churned out of an archaic ice machine. "What mistake did Tom make on this day?"

A few hands shot into the air.

---

15. Staff members at the IFR.

"Mr. Larsson?"

"He didn't have a big enough ice bucket."

"Incorrect."

"Mr. Carmichael?"

"Check out those threads—the man ain't got no style."

"Incorrect." The class cracked up, and even Blaque couldn't help but chuckle. Harold "C-Note" Carmichael, the medical student, had proved to be a formidable Candidate but hadn't lost his knack for keeping it light.

"Mr. Freck?"

"He tried to save the entire World."

"Correct." This was no surprise. It often seemed to the rest of the Candidates that Thibadeau and Fixer Blaque were having an ongoing private conversation that no one else was party to. "Please elaborate for the benefit of the class."

Thibadeau winced, a little uncomfortable at being set apart from his fellows.

"When you're in the middle of a job, you can't start to think about the consequences of your actions, or what might happen to The World if you fail. That can be a very slippery slope, which can only lead to one place . . ."

He turned back to Fixer Jackal, who in his effort to save every single ice cube, was, in fact, saving none.

"*Attaque de panique.*"

"Exactly," agreed Fixer Blaque. "If you try to absorb the entire scope of a problem—if you try to save The World in toto—you will end up saving nothing at all."

Becker offered Thib a covert low-five but yanked it away at the last moment.

"Teacher's pet."

Thibadeau faked a punch, before both of them returned to the lesson.

"Pause sequence!"

The action stopped, leaving the Time Keepers frozen in midstride and Fixer Jackal drowning in a pool of melting Moments.

As with every lesson, Fixer Blaque saved the most valuable part for last.

"In every Mission, there is something small, something you can wrap your heart around, that will grant you the power to transcend the fear." Fixer Blaque called out to the Simulator staff, "Enhance 224 to 176!"

An ice cube on the floor lifted up and expanded to ten times its regular size. Inside were two people kissing in a snow-covered forest on a lost winter day, and the Candidates leaned in for a closer look.

"Find the Mission *inside* the Mission . . ."

Night Watchmen's Station, Department of Sleep, The Seems

". . . and you will have found the greatest Tool of all."

Once again, Becker's Training had paid off and his own "*attaque de panique*" was soon to be under control.

"Keep going . . ."

At the Fixer's request, Night Watchman #1 flipped through the Cases featured on his console: people in varying degrees of distress, all as a result of the Glitch in Sleep.

"I don't understand the point of—"

"Keep going!"

College kids at school. Bedouins inside their tents. And then . . .

"There!"

A girl with dirty blond hair and bright green eyes came up on the screen. She was about the same age as Becker, sitting in her bed and struggling not to cry.

"What's her story?"

With a keystroke, the Night Watchman pulled up her Case File on the screen. It had the seal of the Big Building on the front.

"Jennifer Kaley. Sector 104, Grid 11. I think that's near Toronto."

"Caledon, to be exact." Simly blushed for being a know-it-all.

The Night Watchman seemed troubled as he decompressed the file.

"It looks like a 532 was ordered for her tonight . . ."

"What's a 532?"

"A Dream that only a Case Worker can call in. They use it when nothing else will work."

"Why? What's wrong with her?" asked Becker.

The Night Watchman hit another key, but the computer bleeped "Access Denied."

"Sorry, personal and confidential. You need a clearance level of eight to open that up, and mine's only seven."

"Here, let me try." Fixers have a clearance level of nine-plus (out of a possible eleven), and when Becker typed in his pass code, information began to scroll.

According to her dossier, Jennifer Kaley was being picked

on at school for basically no good reason. There were snapshots of her walking down the halls, being shunned by the other kids. Sitting by herself in the cafeteria. And one really painful clip of her being jeered and mocked when she was just trying to walk home after school, with her head down and her tie-dyed backpack hanging from her side.

"Well, did she get it?" asked Becker.

"Get what?"

"The Dream. Did she get it before the Glitch struck?"

The Watchman surfed and surfed but found only a solitary beep.

"Negative. And there's no way to get it to her unless she falls asleep."

The same hundred pairs of eyes turned to Becker once again, and as he looked at the girl in the window, he finally started to understand what Fixer Blaque had been talking about. Right now, she was forcing a smile so her mom wouldn't worry as much even while wondering how she was going to make it through the next day. Why Becker was drawn to her, he couldn't really say—there were probably bigger Cases in The World that day—but for him, Jennifer Kaley was the Mission Inside the Mission. And that's all he needed to know.

"Let's Fix."

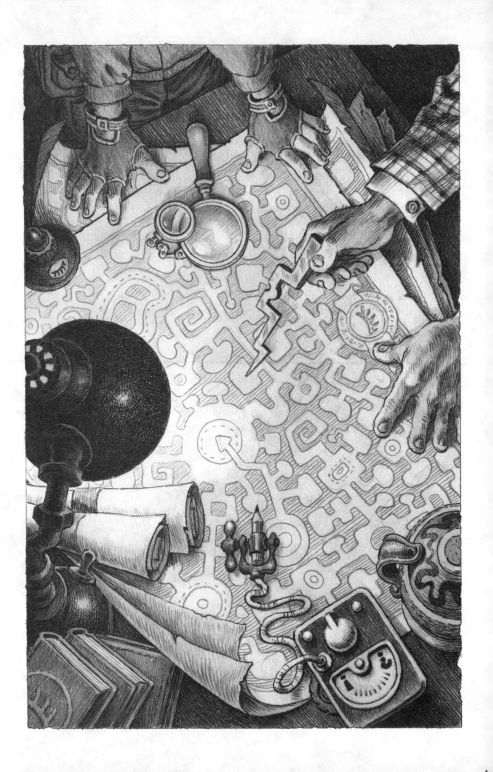

The Slumber Party

Though miniscule in size, Glitches are a Fixer's worst nightmare. They typically pop up in one device, and if left unchecked, can spread across an entire department, eventually resulting in wholesale collapse. Glitches were thought to have been eliminated during "Operation Clean Sweep." It may be impossible to rid the system of what many believe to be the natural outgrowth of any complex machine.

Degree of Difficulty: 10.0

—*The Compendium of Malfunction & Repair, p. 108*

Office of the Foreman, Department of Sleep, The Seems

"No. No. Not that one." The Sleep Foreman shuffled desperately through a dusty file cabinet in his office. "Ah—here we go!"

On his drafting desk, the devoted employee unrolled the

faded blueprints of the famed Department of Sleep. The factory itself was massive and composed of a series of "Bedrooms," each responsible for producing one individual component of Sleep. Yet the layout seemed to defy any known law of physics.

"The guy who designed this place was a freak. His whole concept was that the department should look and feel like a pillow fort."

If that was so, he'd certainly succeeded. There were hallways constructed entirely of blankets and pillows, doorways made of upturned mattresses, and soft, custom-made Night Lights, which cast a soporific atmosphere throughout. In addition, a handful of secret Bedrooms seemed to have no entrance or exit at all.

"Show me the progression of the Glitch," requested Becker.

"The initial Blip was in one of the Rest Areas," reported the Foreman. "But by the time we got there, it had already hit here . . . here . . . and here."

"Whoa, that's fast," Simly marveled.

Unlike Foibles, which tend to pop up in a single machine, unraveling its inner workings but usually staying put, Glitches move from machine to machine, trashing everything in their wake. Becker knew the only way to stop one is to track it down and Fix it, before it does damage beyond repair.

"The last alert was in the Snooze." The Foreman pointed to the location on the map. "But it could be anywhere by now."

"We need to pick up the scent." Becker checked his Time Piece™, then turned to his Briefer. "Recommendation?"

Simly thought it over, then produced several items from his Briefcase.

"Well, you could use a Vindwoturelukinvor™ but those

can be flaky at night. A Wharizit™ is money in the bank . . . oh, wait! I have the perfect thing."

He whipped out a busted-up old Tool. It was caked with dirt and looked like it hadn't been used in years.

"What kind of contraption is that?" asked the Foreman.

"It's a Glitchometer™!"

Glitchometers had been all the rage in the days before Clean Sweep, but they had been discontinued due to serious design flaws and now were mostly collectibles or sold at antique Tool fairs.

"Where on earth did you get it?" asked Becker, impressed.

"I didn't get it on earth! I got it from my grandfather's Toolkit. He's got all kinds of wacky junk." Simly's paternal grandfather was regarded as one of the greatest Briefers who ever lived, and though he had never made it to Fixer, he had assisted on many a famous Mission. Simly fired up the Tool and it sprang to life, the sensitive needle flipping back and forth, before zeroing itself. "Glitchometers focus in directly on the unique energy trail left by a Glitch, and when activated, should take us right—"

But black smoke began to cough out the sides, along with an awful scraping sound, forcing Simly to shut it down before it blew up in his hands.

"Sorry, boss. I don't know what happened." Simly was dejected, especially considering he prided himself on Tool prep and deployment. "Do you want me to call my grandpa and see if he can—"

"Don't sweat it, Simly." Becker rolled up the blueprints and stuffed them in his Toolkit. "We'll do this the old-fashioned way."

Deep in the sub-basement of the factory was where they manufactured Snooze—one of the three key ingredients (along with Refreshment and Twinkle) that were mixed to create Sleep itself. Since this was where the Glitch was last sighted, it was here that Becker and Simly began their investigation.

The air was hot and thick with the smell of burning rubber. Men with smocks and welding visors loaded pure Exhaustion into smelting pots while mechanized arms dropped molasses and maple syrup from gargantuan soup ladles. Once cooled, the gelatinous mess congealed into a thick taffylike substance, which was then cut into chunks and shipped to the Master Bedroom for final mixing.

"No, no, no, no no!" A rosy-cheeked man in a chef's outfit was sampling the batch. "Zis is too sweet!"

The Snoozemaster had been promoted from "Sous" all the way to "Chef de Cuisine" because of his instinct for how to make Sleep even tastier, but his bombastic personality had ruffled a few feathers along the way.

"What do you want from me?" cried one of the Tireless Workers. "The Glitch threw off our entire recipe!"

"Gleech, Gleech, Gleech! I no want to hear no more about zis Gleech!" The Snoozemaster kicked over a row of pots and pans, while beside him, Becker waited patiently for the temper tantrum to subside.

"So tell me again how it started?"

"I get call into ze office, on a night when I have tickets to Ze Snorchestra no less, and what do I findz? All ze recipes for ze Snooze are, how you say, bass ackwards!"

The master pressed the Snooze button and rebooted his computer, which printed Becker a list of recipes that had all been mixed and matched.

"Coffee beans are being blended with Pizzazz. Cinnamon with ze Mope. I told zese idiots from day one not computerize ze cookbooks. We makes zis by hand since back in ze Day, and ze system need no Fixing!"

Becker shook his head. One of the great frustrations of Fixing was the tendency of the Powers That Be to layer "quick fixes" on top of the existing technology, rather than fess up to the need for a page one redesign. "Give me a second, okay?"

"Everybody stand back," announced Briefer Frye. "Give the man some space!"

Becker closed his eyes, and using the old-fashioned way, reached out with his 7th Sense to hone in on the Glitch. Judging from the goose bumps that sprouted up along his arms, he had picked up the trail, but it was still faint.

"I wish I could stay to help rewrite your recipes," apologized Becker, "but I have to get my hands around this thing before it trashes the whole department."

The Snoozemaster understood but still appeared quite shaken.

"But what about ze Snooze? Sleep cannot be mixed wizout ze precious Snooze!"

Becker stepped over to a vat, dipped his finger in the sludge, and took a sample taste.

"It's almost there. Maybe an Energy reduction would enhance the flavor of the underlying Exhaustion?"

"No, no, no. Zis is crazy. It will never work . . ." Simly and the Tireless Workers dropped their eyes to the floor. "Unless . . ."

"A little bit of Love?" Becker seemed to read his mind.

"Exactly!"

A spark shot through the room.

"Can you do it in time?" the Fixer asked hopefully.

"Not only can I," bellowed the Snoozemaster, turning toward his line cooks with fire in his eyes. "But it shall be ze heaviest, most satisfying Snooze anyone in Ze World has ever seen!"

A roar went up among the Tireless Workers, but as they scrambled to gather the necessary ingredients, Simly couldn't resist taking a taste for himself.

"Needs paprika."

WDOZ, Department of Sleep, The Seems

"W...D...O...Zzzzzzzzzz."

Becker's goose bumps had led them to a small radio station on the roof of the department and while the jingle lingered in the air, he and Simly waited for the disc jockey to finish up his act.

"And that was 'The Sound of Rain Outside Your Window on a Lazy Afternoon,' by the Somnambulists . . . an oldie but goodie, *designed* to ease your *mind* into the soft, sweet paradise of Sleep."

WDOZ had been established to broadcast soft tones to the subconscious minds of the people of The World—helping them to relax in preparation for the arrival of their Good Night's Sleep. The DJ pulled another forty-five from the library in the booth.

"Up next, I've got a fresh take on a deep cut from back in the Day . . ." He put the needle to the record, which was entitled

"The Hum of the Air Conditioner (Remix)." "My name is Johnny Zzzzzzzzzzz and you've been listening to WDOZ, greasing the hinges on the ol' inner doorway since 13303."

As the record began to spin, the balding, pony-tailed jock lowered the volume and exited the booth to join Becker and Simly.

"Look, brother"—his off-air personality was a far cry from his on-air one—"I don't know what anyone told you, but there ain't no Glitch in *my* station."

"I'm not here to blame anybody," Becker assured him. "It's just that Glitches can be tricky. Maybe it got into the board."

"A Glitch got into the board?" The DJ shook his head, insulted, then pulled out a pair of headphones and jacked them into the slot. "Be my guest."

Becker gave Simly the okay to put the phones on, and Johnny Z cranked up the volume on what was being broadcast to The World that very moment. In a matter of seconds, Simly's eyelids started to get heavy and he began to make space for himself on the floor.

"See? The Z-man never fails."

This guy reminded Becker of Joel Waldman—a kid from Highland Park who had a major attitude problem—but the Fixer still wasn't convinced. He reached into his Toolkit and pulled out a dog-eared copy of the one book that every Fixer cannot do without.

Its official name was *The Compendium of Malfunction & Repair,* but everyone who had one called it "the Manual" and (as promised in the foreword) it contained "Everything You Need to Know to Fix." Becker turned to chapter 6, "Schematics and Blueprints," and quickly found the page for WDOZ.

"Can I take a look at the Incapacitator?"

"What the heck is that?" The Z-man may have been the Program Director, but he obviously had no clue about the inner workings.

"It's the node that translates your records into frequencies that people in The World can hear."

"Just make it quick, bro. I got a show to run here."

Following the Manual's instructions, Becker flipped open the board and tunneled his way to the core of the circuitry. In the middle of a bunch of tangled wires was a small transistor, through which all of WDOZ's signals had to travel. Just as he had suspected, it was burned to a crisp and Becker bypassed the hub to reveal what was actually being piped out to audiences worldwide.

"Ahhh!" Simly yanked off the headphones, suddenly wide awake. "It sounds like grinding gears mixed with a screaming baby cow."

"I wish I could say I was surprised," said Fixer Drane. "Only one thing could have done this kind of damage in that amount of time . . . but it's already long gone."

Johnny Z looked contrite and tried to pull his tail from between his legs.

"Do you think you can Fix it?"

Cafeteria, Department of Sleep, The Seems

Becker skillfully replaced the toasted Incapacitator with the newer, faster Zonker 111, but the Glitch had not stopped there. It was cutting a swath through the entire department, jumping from Bedroom to Bedroom and machine to machine, and each of the elements of Sleep was beginning to break down.

Fresh-baked Yawns were coming out of the oven, yet they had failed to adequately rise. Wake-Up Calls were being sent too early, Bedtime Stories were churned out with little or no Inspiration, and the Sack was being hit to virtually no effect at all. Even Pillow Frosting was coating the other side of people's pillows with Hot instead of Cool.

Along the way, Becker and Simly were Fixing like madmen, but this was the rub of hunting a Glitch: the subtle and complex trail of devastation it left behind could only be handled by a Fixer (and Briefer), yet the attention that had to be given to that trail made it nearly impossible to gain any ground.

Exhausted and soaked with sweat, the partners took a break at the Employee Cafeteria, where three Wake-Up Call Operators were comforting each other after having come face-to-face with the nasty root of all the evening's troubles.

"It was terrible," cried a blue-haired old lady. "It blew up my entire switchboard."

Her friends nodded sadly and brushed the ash from their coworker's frazzled bouffant.

"There, there, Shirley. A Fixer is here now and it'll all be over soon."

Becker and Simly glanced at each other, then immediately got back to business.

"I still don't understand why it doesn't work." The Glitcho-meter was splayed out on the lunch table before them.

"Don't worry about it," answered Becker, rereading the "Bleeps, Blips, and Blunders" chapter of his Manual for any clues on how to proceed. "And eat your midnight snack, cause we're gonna need all the energy we can get once we find this thing."

Simly nodded and pulled out a brown paper bag that had been packed by his mom. There were carrots and celery wrapped in plastic, hardboiled eggs, and even a slice of Dazzleberry Pie.[16]

"So how does it feel to finally make it to Fixer?"

"Pretty cool, I guess." Becker took a bite of his PowerBar and continued to leaf through the text. "A little more pressurized, though."

Simly was in the mood to chat (as usual) but Becker had larger things on his mind—not least of which was his gnawing concern over whether this was another offensive by The Tide. A recent memo from Central Command had warned all Fixers about the growing dangers of this insurrection, and Becker ran down the list of recent strikes in his mind. This incident certainly bore similarities to the night a horde of fruit flies was unleashed into the Grapevine, shorting out interdepartmental communications, but The Tide always left its calling card— the symbol of the black cresting wave—and, as of yet, no such thing had been found.

"I want to be a Fixer someday."

"What was that?"

16. The "Dazzleberry" was scrapped back in the Day by the Food & Drink Administration (FDA) for allegedly being "too sweet" (and tasty).

"I said I want to be a Fixer too. Like you."

"You do?"

This was surprising to Becker because Simly was born in The Seems, and though humans and Seemsians are similar in almost every regard, they differ in one important detail. Seemsians aren't born with a Fixer's greatest asset, a 7th Sense, which is why they almost always top out at Briefer.

"Yeah, I know there's the whole 7th Sense issue . . . but my grandpa always said I was gonna be the first one in the family to make it all the way."

"Well, you're very good at what you do, that's for sure. And as far as the 7th Sense thing goes, did you ever read *The Journal of Al Penske*?"

"You mean the Toolmaster?" asked Simly. "Yeah, I read it. But there's nothing in there about—"

"If you look in appendix C, he tells this really cool story about how he found his 7th Sense by pretending he was born in The World and visualizing how he might feel if 'something was wrong' in The Seems."

"Really?" Simly's eyes brightened up momentarily. "Have you ever heard of that actually working?"

"No. But that doesn't mean it's not worth a shot."

Becker could tell that Simly wasn't quite buying it but that he appreciated the gesture nonetheless.

"Can I ask you one more thing, sir?"

It was still kind of weird for Becker to be referred to as "sir," especially by someone fifteen years older than he.

"Call me Becker, Sim."

"That girl in Sector 104?"

"Jennifer Kaley?"

"Yeah. How come you chose her to be your Mission Inside the Mission? Instead of all the other Cases?"

Becker thought it over. Of course Jennifer's situation was compelling and she was pretty and all that, but it was more just the feeling he got when he saw her. Sometimes things like that are hard to put into words, and usually best left that way.

"I don't know. There was just something about her." Becker looked up at Simly. "Why, who would you have chosen?"

"I think the guy in the motel. The salesman. I just really hope he gets home in time for his daughter's birthday."

"Then you can Fix for him and I can Fix for her. Cool?"

"Cool."

They each packed up their Toolkit and Briefcase respectively, then Becker took a peek at the clock on the cafeteria wall.

"C'mon, I think I've got an idea . . ."

Pillowstone Lane, Department of Sleep, The Seems

On the east side of Sleep, near Shuteye's Shoe Repair, was a small nightclub that had become an institution in The Seems. Here, people from every department would gather to blow off steam, and Becker thought he might be able to find someone in the Know.

"I don't know about this, sir."

"Shhhh!"

Becker and Simly were peering out of a fire exit and into the dark alley. Mist filled the air and an old Tinker pushed a cart down an uneven cobblestone road.

"They'll find her someday . . . they'll bring her back . . ." His cart was filled with sleep masks, earplugs, and even a Craftmatic adjustable bed. "The Plan is good . . . the Plan is good."

The Tinker disappeared into the fog, leaving only one other sign of life in the alley: a broken-down neon marquee, which swung back and forth on a single rusty hinge.

The Slmb r P a ty

"We can't go in there," whispered Simly.

"Why not?"

"My mom says it's a really rough joint."

"Don't worry. I got your back."

Beneath the sign was a muscular Bouncer, dressed all in black, and reading a copy of the *Daily Plan*.[17] An underage student from the School of Thought was trying to con her way in, but he didn't even look up from the crossword.

"But I don't have a fake ID," Simly worried.

"You don't need one, you're twenty-seven."

"Oh yeah."

"Besides, we've got something much better than a fake ID."

---

17. The leading newspaper in The Seems, including politics, World news, sports, arts & entertainment, the classifieds, and *The Jinx Gnomes*—a popular comic strip about the crack unit dispatched to The World whenever a person overcelebrates a bit of good fortune.

Simly and Becker crossed the street and flashed the Fixer's Badge. The Bouncer held it up to the light, making sure it was legit, than stamped both their hands and lifted the velvet rope.

"Why do *they* get to go in?" cried the teenage girl, still stuck out in the cold.

"Because," said the Bouncer, filling in 32 Across.[18]

The inside of the Slumber Party was barely illuminated by gas-lit Night Lights, scattered one to a table. Smoke filled the air and Seemsians from every department sat in booths and alcoves, drinking multicolored elixirs and speaking in hushed tones. Becker and Simly made their way past the band in the corner—a three-piece jazz ensemble that laid down a drowsy groove—and approached the mahogany bar.

"Can I help you, gentlemen?"

The bartender, who, judging by the tattoos on his arm, was a veteran of the Color Wars, seemed amused by the appearance of a twelve-year-old boy with a Tool-covered dork in tow.

"We're looking for someone in The Know."

Becker flashed his Badge again, hoping the barkeep could put him in touch with one of The Seems's most infamous secret societies—a criminal element that traded in Plan-sensitive information.

"Wish I could help you boys, but I ain't never heard of no Know."

"Listen, bubba." Becker had no choice but to play hardball.

---

18. Four letters: Aka "The Time Bandits," Justin and _ _ _ _ F. Time.

He leaned over the bar and pressed his nose right up against the larger man's face. "You know there's a Know and I know there's a Know and we both know The Know is known to hang out here."

The bartender stared back, giving him nothing at all.

"So unless you want me to bring my boys from the FDA down here and have them find out what you're *really* serving, you better start singing, and I mean *now!*"

Simly couldn't believe what Becker was saying to this big, burly dude. After all, the kid could barely see over the bar to even talk to him. But he supposed that's part of what made Becker a Fixer.

"Check out the VIP area." The barkeep finally gave in. "Maybe you'll find what you're looking for back there."

As he walked away muttering, Becker winked at Simly, then gave him the bad news.

"Listen, Sim. We're gonna need to split up."

"We are?"

"Yeah, I need to be able to fit in a little better." Becker pulled off his Badge and messed up his hair with a handful of Goop™. "Just stay here and see what you can find."

"No problem."

"And Sim?"

"Yeah?"

"Try to be cool."

"Cool? I'm cool." Simly was deeply offended. "Cool's my middle name."

They gave each other the Shake,[19] then Becker disappeared

---

19. The IFR secret handshake, taught only to Candidates who have successfully passed the Practical.

into the throng. But as the Briefer turned around, he could feel the eyes of the entire club upon him.

"Correction," he said to himself, reminded of the day he walked out at the YMSA pool without his bathing suit on. "My middle name is not cool. It's Alomonus."

In the back of the club was the cordoned-off VIP area, and Becker was able to slide through gracefully under his new cover as a hip young Case Worker on the go. No one questioned his credentials, simply by the way he carried himself and how he dropped bits of information that only someone who worked at the Big Building would ever know.

"So, anyway, I'm working on this love story between two people in Sector 906 and the whole thing depends on this woman getting a GNS, and boom! A Glitch puts the kibosh on the whole thing."

"Yeah, I heard about that," said a curious Cloud Picker. "Word is they brought in a Fixer."

"Those guys get all the good gigs," pretended Becker.

"Not to mention all the credit."

A lot of employees resented the appearance of a Fixer because it tacitly implied that they weren't capable of handling the job themselves. Becker let it go and was about to prod him for more info when there was a tug on the back of his shirt.

"You know all about that, don't you, Fixer boy?" Standing behind him was a Flavor Miner, smears of Chocolate Chip Mint and Butter Pecan still on his oversized smock.

"What do you mean, Fixer boy?" asked the Picker.

"This guy's a company man all the way."

Becker was scrambling to save face as a crowd started to gather.

"Listen bro, I was just tryin' to—"

"We don't like your kind in here," coughed an unemployed Wordsmith, and a few Time Flies chimed in, working up the crowd into an angry froth.

"I'm not looking for any trouble."

"Well it's looking for *you*."

Becker sized up the enemy and wished for a moment that he hadn't given his Toolkit to Simly for safekeeping.

"*Le partir seul!*"

A voice rang out from the midst of the shadows, and everyone turned to see the source: an edgy-looking guy in a suede jacket and Serengetti shades, sitting in a back booth all alone.

"I'll take care of this one myself."

Whoever he was, the guy commanded respect, because the crowd instantly dispersed. Becker was about to say thanks, when he was stunned to see who had rescued him from the mob.

A little older, shaggier, and more grizzled. But definitely someone he knew.

"Thibadeau?"

Thibadeau Freck

The Stumbling Block, Institute for Fixing & Repair,
The Seems—One Year Ago

"You're shanking it, Draniac!"

Becker looked over to Thibadeau Freck, his heart racing and sweat dripping in his eyes.

"Shank this, Napoleon!"

The two Candidates had reached the ninth (and final) level of the Stumbling Block—the IFR's infamous obstacle course—and now stood side by side, desperately trying to untie their Gordian Knot before the other did.

"This is what I love about you Americans," jibed Thib, testing the thick ball of interwoven rope with his fingers. "You put ketchup on your fries, you have bad cheese and even worse coffee, and *still* you never give up!"

The wind at this height whipped across their faces, making

it even more difficult to see what they were doing. The Stumbling Block was built like a wedding cake, with concentric circular platforms stacked on top of each other, each containing a unique Fixing challenge. Every Friday, the Candidates would face hurdles as disparate as Number Crunching to getting out from under an Impression, and as usual, Freck and Drane were first and second in the race up to the top. In recent weeks, however, the gap between them had begun to close.

"This reminds me of making monkey's fists at camp!" Becker studied his own ball of rope, a simulation of the real Gordian Knot, which in Reality held together both ends of the Spectrum. "And if I just do *this* . . ."

Becker "pulled the rabbit through the hole" (as his waterfront director David Lincoln had taught him to do), unraveling a large chunk of the cord—and for the first time ever, took a narrow lead over his closest friend in Training.

"*Sacre bleu!*" exclaimed Thibadeau, still perplexed by his own tangled mess. Adrenaline coursed through Becker as he realized that triumph was almost within his grasp.

"I would say congratulations to you"—the Frenchman almost seemed ready to concede—"but if I just do *this* . . ."

At the bottom of the tangle, Thibadeau gave a single thread the gentlest of tugs, and all at once, his entire knot unraveled.

"Catch you on the Flip Side, *mon ami!*"

With a wink, Thibadeau scrambled up the ladder and disappeared to the top of the Block. Becker's heart sank, but he managed to pull himself together, for he didn't want to be overtaken by any of the other Candidates (who were no doubt right on his heels) and besides, how you handle defeat can be just as important as how you handle victory.

"Always the bridesmaid, never the bride," said Fixer Blaque, who was waiting for Becker when at last he reached the top.

"Yes, sir. I really thought I had him this time."

The best part of the Stumbling Block was the finish—win or lose, you ended on a roof deck stocked with snacks, beverages, and some of the tastiest views in The Seems. Blaque was already preparing the end-of-the-week feast on a charcoal grill for his exhausted Candidates, while Thib was lazing back and forth in a hammock, peeling a clementine.

"You did have me, Draniac." Thibadeau handed a slice to the depleted Becker. "The Agents of L.U.C.K. were just on my side today."

That was the cool thing about his rivalry with Thibadeau— no matter how hard they fought (and they fought hard), it never got in the way of their friendship. Becker grabbed the nearest hammock and positioned himself in the center of the netting. For a few tranquil moments, they just looked out at The Seems.

"Draniac, can I ask you something?"

"Yeah, man." Becker jumped at the chance because Thib had never come to him for advice before. "Anything."

"Do you ever wonder . . . ," the Frenchman lowered his voice as if he didn't want Fixer Blaque to hear, "why they made The World the way it is?"

"What do you mean?"

"I mean, do you ever think that maybe they could have done a better job?"

Becker wasn't sure how to reply. He was still in awe of the very existence of The Seems, so he had never really thought much about it.

"Better? How much better could it be?"

"I don't know, dude. It just seems like a lot of things are wrong. Like hurricanes or this kid I saw at Charles De Gaulle airport a couple days ago who could barely talk because he had some terrible disease." Thib's eyes wandered to the Big Building, which towered through the clouds in the distance. "I wonder why they let those kinds of things happen."

"I don't know." Becker struggled to find the right thing to say. "I guess it's all part of the Plan?"

"Yeah, you're right. That must be it." Thibadeau shrugged it off like it was no big deal. "Hey, look—here comes the Swede!"

They leaned over the side to see Candidate Larsson arriving at the Knot in third place, and exhorted him to pick up the pace. In the back of Becker's mind, Thibadeau's question lingered, but he figured they'd have more than enough time to talk about such heady topics.

He figured wrong.

Office of the Instructor, IFR, The Seems— Nearly Eight Months Ago

Fixer Blaque's office was the most coveted space in the entire IFR, mostly because this was where Jayson once sat. Behind a rich mahogany desk, a slew of plaques and Golden Wrenches were posted on the walls, along with photographs of some of the most famous Fixers of all time. There was Blaque with Greg the

Journeyman, with the Octogenarian, with Morgan Asher, and the Instructor looked up at them from his chair, wishing one of his peers could do what he had to do next.

"Come in, Candidate Drane."

Becker stood in the doorway in his IFR warm-ups, soaked in sweat. He had just come off the Beaten Track, when one of the Mechanics had delivered the devastating news.

"When did it happen?"

"Last night. Twenty-seven hundred hours." Blaque leaned back in his chair, weighing his words carefully. He had been through a lot of conversations like this in the past, but it never got any easier. "They tried their best to pull him out, but this is all that's left."

On top of the desk was a box of personal effects. A Manual. A Toolkit stained with Tears of Joy. And a black IFR bandanna, salt where the sweat had once been. A label on the cardboard flap said it all: THIBADEAU FRECK.

"I informed the rest of the class this morning. You're the last to know."

Becker searched for any sign of grief in Fixer Blaque's face. After all, Thib had been his prize pupil. But, as always, the tell-tale blue shades concealed all.

"Thank you for telling me, sir."

"Sit down, Becker."

"That's okay, sir. I was just gonna hit the show—"

"Sit down."

Becker took a seat in the brown leather chair. He tried to keep his emotions in check, but for the first time since Orientation, he felt like exactly what he was: a boy in a World he didn't understand.

"It's not always easy to be part of this thing." Fixer Blaque motioned with his hands, as if to imply The World and The Seems and everything In-Between. "Sometimes things will happen and you'll start to wonder, is there really any Plan? Or is it just wishful thinking—a convenient delusion I've invented for myself?"

Becker nodded, though he didn't hear a thing. His eyes absently wandered to an old sepia picture of a younger Blaque, with Lisa Simms and Tom Jackal, geared up and about to hop on a train. He wondered what Mission this was and why Blaque wasn't wearing his glasses, which he'd never seen him without.

"At times like this, there's only one thing we can fall back on . . ."

Fixer Blaque picked up Thibadeau's Badge, which had melted into a jagged square.

"Our faith."

But right now, Becker was far too angry to be comforted by another one of his Instructor's famous lessons. Thib was the best friend he'd had since Amy Lannin died, and now he was gone too.

"Faith in what, Fixer Blaque?" Becker's eyes began to tear. "Faith in what?"

The Slumber Party, Department of Sleep,
The Seems—Now

"Dude, I can't believe it!"

Becker shook Thibadeau by the collar, as if trying to convince himself that what he was seeing was real. "You're still—"

"Alive?" Thibadeau smiled at his friend's exuberance. "And kicking."

After a few more shakes, Becker finally let go, and he joined the Frenchman at the private table. The sounds of the Slumber Party quickly dropped away, muted by the violet curtains that hung over the alcove.

"Fixer Blaque said you had fallen into a Well of Emotion and they couldn't get you out and . . . and . . . this is great!"

"Nice Badge." Thibadeau took a sip from his glass and eased back into the shadows. "Did anybody else make it?"

"Not yet. But C-Note and Von Schroëder are close."

"Von Schroëder? Wow, that's a dark horse call. I would have put my euros on the Swede."

"The Swede?" Becker smiled. "That's a Story for Another Day."

There was an awkward silence and the young Fixer started to feel uncomfortable. Back at the IFR, when he and Thibadeau had been best friends, there was a certain *je ne sais quoi* about the Frenchman. An aura that when you stepped inside of it, made you feel special too. But that feeling had shifted somehow. Now, Becker almost felt a little scared; that same five o'clock shadow and secondhand jacket that had once made Thib so stylish and suave had taken on a very sinister edge.

"Why didn't you Blink me or get in touch?" Becker tried not to look hurt, but he obviously was. "I mean, I thought you were—"

"Sorry, *mon frére*. I know I should have called. But there were things going on that I couldn't speak to you about."

"Like what?"

A waitress passed by carrying a tray of multicolored liquids. "Truth Serum, Love Potion, Nectar of the Gods?"

"Not tonight, honey." Thibadeau waited for her to leave. "Do you want the truth or do you want me to candy-coat it?"

"What do you think?" Becker was insulted that he even had to ask.

"It's hard to explain. I loved Fixing, you know I did. But there were some things that just didn't . . . make sense." Thibadeau idly fiddled with his Slumber Party matchbook. "Remember that time on the Block? When I asked you about The World being better than it was?"

"Yeah?"

"Well, it was just a feeling back then, but I couldn't shake the questions. If The World was so great then why were there all these problems? Why were the Powers That Be letting it happen?"

"Everybody has those questions," admitted Becker.

"Well, I had to find out the answers." The saxophonist kicked into his solo, and Thibadeau took a moment to appreciate the jam. "Fixer Blaque couldn't give them to me, so finally I went to the Big Building, but all they did was spew out the usual mumbo jumbo about how 'everything happens for a reason,' and 'you can't have the good without the bad.' I just couldn't accept that anymore . . ."

The crowd applauded as the band wrapped up their second set.

"That's why I had to bail on the IFR—to search for why. That whole Well of Emotion thing was a setup. I had to make it look like something had happened to me or I would've been 'humanely unremembered,' if you catch my drift."

Becker didn't know what to say.

"But . . . but you were the best."

"At what? Fixing something that was broken beyond repair?" The older of the two shook his head. "I needed something that I knew beyond a Shadow of a Doubt was worth fighting for. And it wasn't the so-called Plan."

Becker was starting to feel sick inside.

"Then what was it?"

Thibadeau reached beneath his shirt and pulled out a silver necklace with a black talisman dangling from the end. Etched on to the pendant was the image of a wave, foaming and about to crash down upon the shore.

"I think you already know the answer to that."

Back at the bar, Simly had busted out his Briefing pad and was conducting random interviews. Right now he was in the process of interrogating a large, hairy guy in a tutu.

"So, let me get this straight—you're a Tooth Fairy?"

"Yeah, you got a problem with that?"

"No, I just always thought that was a trick parents in The World played on their kids."

The Fairy rolled his eyes, as if this was a common (yet irksome) misperception.

"Nowadays it is. But once upon a time, we used to do it, and let me tell you—we got respect. Then Collections got combined with Lost and Found and we got squeezed out. Don't even know who I am anymore."

"Bummer." Simly could almost feel his sorrow. "Maybe you should go back and get another degree . . ."

"It's too late for me, man. Once you've had the thrill of pickin' a lock on a window, grabbin' that tooth, and leavin' a silver dollar for a kid under his pillow? Knowin' he's gonna wake up in the morning and say, 'Mom, the Tooth Fairy came!'—well, there just ain't no place to go after that."

The Tooth Fairy shook his head, lost in the wistful memory, then threw back another Shot in the Dark.

"But enough about me. How can I help you, chief?"

"Well," said Simly, dropping his voice to a whisper, "it's about this Glitch . . ."

The crowd in the VIP room had begun to build, despite the argument that was heating up in the corner.

"We don't want to destroy The World." Thibadeau pounded his fist on the table, his voice infused with the fervor of a true believer. "We want to save it!"

"Is that what you were doing when you poked holes in the Bags of Wind?" Becker yelled back. "Or what about the Rain Tower—I could've been killed on that Mission."

"We tried a peaceful solution a long time ago, but the Powers That Be refuse to listen. So now we have to take matters into our own hands."

"But what about the damage to The World?"

"Change always comes with a price. One day, when everything is different, you'll see that it was worth it."

Thibadeau pointed Becker's attention to a huge flat-screen Window, where images from The World were being projected as part of the club's funky ambience.

"The World is a lost cause, Becker." At that moment, an image of an orphan flashed upon the screen, crying and wandering through the streets of Rio de Janeiro. "What kind of Plan allows for something like that?"

Becker stared up at the child, who slowly dissolved into an exploding volcano.

"Once it might have worked, but suffering is an old idea. It doesn't do anybody any good, so why is it still here? Because the Plan fell apart long ago." Thib's hand found its way to his pendant. "If there ever was a Plan at all."

Becker was thunderstruck. During Training, Thibadeau had often mused about the beautiful intricacies of the Plan.

"Our time is coming, Becker. We've infiltrated every department, every corner of The Seems, and when the word is given, the Tide will rise and seize the means of production to make a better world. A perfect world." For a moment, Thibadeau's expression softened, and Becker felt like he was back with his old friend. "Join us, Draniac. I promise, it'll be sweet."

Becker considered his classmate's offer. Of course he had his own doubts—everybody did, and it was tempting. Especially when things in The World didn't always make sense and it seemed so easy for The Seems to change them. But Becker had also made a choice . . .

"The beauty of The World is how it is, Thib. Not how it isn't."

Thibadeau fell back into his chair.

"Blaque really got to you good, didn't he?"

"I guess so."

"I'm sorry it had to be this way." Thibadeau looked like he genuinely meant it. "The Tide could use a man like you."

"Well, at least I know where the Glitch came from."

Thibadeau laughed out loud.

"Please—we would never unleash something that impossible to control. Besides, when we make our next move, you'll know it. And you won't have to ask who's responsible."

Becker felt his ire rising but kept it in check, because the Mission had to come first.

"Is there anything you can tell me? For old time's sake?"

Thibadeau thought it over long and hard, then pulled out a ballpoint pen.

"I can only tell you what I heard under the Radar." He finished writing and handed Becker the matchbook he'd been fiddling with. "But next time we see each other . . . it won't be the same."

Becker got up and flipped a coin into the open guitar case in front of the band.

"It already isn't."

Freight Elevator 3, Department of Sleep, The Seems

Simly and Becker were cruising in a freight elevator toward the upstairs Bedrooms of Sleep. And though the Mission was still very much in jeopardy, the Fixer seemed dazed and out of it.

"You're wrong," he whispered. "That's not the way it is . . ."

"Excuse me, sir?"

Becker had been rattled by his encounter with Thibadeau

and had nearly forgotten where he was and what he was doing there.

"Sir?"

"Sorry, Simly." He shook off the lingering taste of the argument. "Go ahead with your report."

"Well, I did get one decent tip." Simly pulled out his Briefing pad, which was filled with scribbles from his conversation with the Tooth Fairy. "According to my informant, this Glitch seems to have a . . .'mind of its own.' "

"What's that supposed to mean?"

"Glitches usually move in random patterns, right? And destroy everything in their path?"

"Yeah . . ."

"But this one's sneakier than that. The breakdowns it's causing are almost impossible to detect, and they get slightly more destructive with each Bedroom that it hits."

Becker couldn't help but agree and it troubled him deeply. A Glitch with a purpose was almost too terrible to contemplate.

"My guy says this is just how it happened during the Not-So-Great Depression.[20]"

"Who Fixed on that one?"

"No one. They say that at the last possible moment, the Glitch just . . . vanished."

Simly tried to moisten his mouth with a piece of Trouble Gum™, but it did little to quell the rising panic.

---

20. A period in the early 1990s when an abundance of Depression was accidentally released during a pipeline break in the Department of Thought & Emotion—the repercussions of which are still being felt to this day.

"How about you, sir? Did you find anything out?"

Becker nodded and handed him the torn-up matchbook. On the inside fold was written a single word:

Dreamatorium

"This is where the Glitch is going next."

Back in The World

12 Grant Avenue, Highland Park, New Jersey

The rings of Saturn glowed a fluorescent green on the ceiling above Benjamin Drane's race-car bed. Jupiter was its big old self, but Mars was actually in the wrong place, located right on the outskirts of Pluto. There was also a spaceship that came with the set and Benjamin had pasted it up there, presuming that this was a family searching for a home on some distant planet, complete with the young daydreaming daughter, adventurous boy, and intrepid parents who would someday arrive and plant their flag of dreams.

Benjamin wasn't used to being up this late, but there was a secret thrill in it. The planets seemed a little brighter and the outside seemed a little darker and the house seemed a little bit—

CREAK.

Something made a sound from inside his closet door.

Benjamin sat up with a start and waited for another sound, which never followed. But it was enough to tweak his mind, which immediately raced toward thoughts of the Boogeyman and *Piñata* (this movie he watched on USA one night) and eventually sent the young boy out of his bed and into the hallway once again.

He had already exhausted his video game collection, and the bathroom held little comfort, so the choice had come down to his parents or his older brother. He knew what he would get from his mom—a long, though loving, digression on the fact that he was just displacing his deeper fears of intimacy, loneliness, and death. And his dad, a professor at Rutgers University, would do just the opposite, taking a hasty trip to the closet and giving Benjamin scientific proof, right there and then, that there was no such monster in attendance.

Benjamin slowly turned the doorknob to his brother's room instead.

"Becker?" He had been reprimanded in the past and agreed (under oath) never to enter Becker's room without written permission, but tonight he was hoping for a reprieve. "Are you awake?"

All that Benjamin got back was the sound of snoring, so he slowly padded across the floor toward his brother's bed.

"Becker . . . I need your help."

Miraculously, the sound waves containing the word "help" flowed out of Benjamin's mouth, through the air, into the auditory canal of the sleeping Me-2, where they were detected by a miniature microphone that activated the settings on the back of its neck, turning the dial automatically from "Sleep" to "Auto-Pilot" without the slightest click.

"Becker, wake up!"

Benjamin reached for what he assumed to be his brother's shoulder when—

"Don't you know I have a quiz tomorrow?" Benjamin nearly jumped out of his skin as the Me-2 rolled over and opened its eyes. "If I blow another one, Mom is gonna kill me!"

Its voice and appearance were indistinguishable from Becker's, and it even seemed to have the same personality.

"But I still can't sleep," cried Benjamin. The younger Drane was on the verge of tears, partially from being afraid to go back into his bedroom and partially from the worst bout of insomnia he had ever experienced. The Me-2 sighed and tapped the side of the mattress.

"C'mere, buddy."

Benjamin wiped away his tears and climbed aboard, his feet barely able to touch the floor.

"I'm gonna tell you something confidential," whispered the look-alike, "but you have to promise not to tell a soul."

"Cross my heart and hope to die."

The Me-2 looked around for effect, as if to make sure no one else could hear.

"It's not just you who can't sleep, B. It's everyone in The World." It opened the shades and the lights of the unsleeping neighborhood showered in. "A Glitch broke out in the Department of Sleep but there's a Fixer on the job and he's one of the best."

Benjamin understood and this brought comfort to his worried mind.

"Is there anything I can do to help?"

"As a matter of fact there is." The Me-2 thought it over. "Go back to your room and draw the coolest picture you can imagine of the Glitch being Fixed—just to give the guy in charge a little extra support. 'Cause trust me, he can feel it!"

Benjamin now had a mission of his own and promptly saluted.

"Aye aye, sir!"

"And when you're done with that, tuck yourself in and await further instructions."

As the boy bolted from the room and back into his own bedroom, the Me-2 cracked a smile.

"That's why they pay me the big bucks."

But that smile faded when the Me-2 glanced out the window once again and saw that the situation had deteriorated even further. Literally every house in the neighborhood was ablaze with light and activity, while out in front of 12 Grant Avenue, Paul the Wanderer had become the first person in recorded history to finish *War and Peace* in a single session, and had gone back to his old habits of wandering the streets unhinged.

"C'mon, Becker. Don't chunk this one."

It was about to lie down and click itself back into "Sleep" mode when the fiber optics implanted in its eye noticed something sitting on the tiny bedside table: Becker's copy of *I Am the Cheese*.

It picked up the book and began to read.

Motel Emmaus, Ulyanovsk, Russia

The TV remote control didn't work and the rooms were still wood-paneled, but the small motel was clean and the staff friendly and courteous. Anatoly sat back on the bed and struggled to take off his shoes. His back was killing him after forty straight hours on the road, and all the travel had worn him to the bone.

"Please, *lapuchka*." He waited patiently as the phone rang one time after another. "Pick up the phone."

Anatoly Nikolievich Svar had been the king of the Northwest Territories only ten years ago, when Formica cabinets had been all the rage and people had a little extra money to spare. But now, with kitchen styles shifting back toward antique woods and purse strings pulled tight, his numbers had become harder and harder to make.

"Hello?" asked the tired voice on the other end of the line. "Is that you, *zaychik*?"

"Did I wake you?"

"No, no . . . I'm still up. How is the trip going?"

"Good, good, things are turning around." He didn't want his wife to worry, so he tried to sugar-coat it. "People are really liking the new line."

"That's wonderful," replied Irina. "I'm so happy for you."

"Is everything ready for tomorrow?"

"All ready. The balloons are up and the cake is in the fridge. Pyotr's coming and he says he's even going to dress up like a clown."

"Let's hope he doesn't scare anyone."

They both laughed at the thought of her brother with greasepaint on his face.

"Well, don't tell Katrina I'm coming, because I want it to be a surprise."

"Are you sure? I don't you want you driving if you're over-tired."

"Don't worry, I'll get at least six hours of sleep before I hit the road." The salesman needed it too, because he had eight more hours to go to make the trip home. "Wait till she sees what I got for her."

At the foot of the bed was a big box wrapped in white paper, with a pink bow taped across the top. It had taken him weeks to find the perfect gift, but it had almost called out to him on the side of the road at a garage sale in Dimitrovgrad.

"Just promise me you'll get some rest," implored Irina.

"I promise. You as well."

"I love you, Anatoly Nikolievich."

"I love you too, Irinochka."

As he hung up the phone, the salesman in the small motel smiled at the thought of his little daughter's face when she opened up the box. No matter what hardships he faced on the road, all that mattered were his precious "girls," and making it home for Katrina's sixth birthday meant the world.

Now if he could only get some sleep.

Levent Business District, Istanbul, Turkey

"Yes, Mr. Demirel, I should have the plans for you by the end of the week, and I will certainly fax them over to you. Yes, me too. Thank you, sir."

Dilara Saffet hung up the phone and shut off the light that illuminated her drafting table, then stepped out onto the busy streets of Istanbul. Cars shared the same roads as pushcarts and carriages, while glittering hotels rose among stone spires and minarets. This was what Dilara loved about this city, the curious blend of old and new, and the ten million people stuck in between.

"Dilara! Dilara! Come! Come!"

The old kerchiefed woman who sold flowers to passersby had become something of a friend to the young architect, and Dilara always made sure to buy at least a tulip from her cart.

"Hello, Mrs. Madakbas. How goes business today?"

"Forget about that. I have something special for you!" The merchant reached into one of her many pockets and pulled out a small piece of blue glass attached to a leather cord. "This will help you find a husband at last!"

Dilara laughed, recognizing the *nazar boncuk*, a local charm that some believed could ward off "evil eyes" and bring about good fortune. Apparently, Mrs. Madakbas thought this might end her terminal singledom and make a good Turkish woman out of her after all.

"I would never argue with you, *babaane!*" Dilara took the charm and put it around her neck. "Because you are always right!"

She kissed the old lady's fingers, then made her way toward the bus stop. Life was not bad for Dilara by any stretch. She had everything a person could ask for—health, a good family and friends, and a career in the process of taking off. But still, she had never met the right person to share it with.

"I must be happy for what I have," she told herself when the thoughts came back on lonely afternoons, but she wasn't getting any younger. And when her parents asked when they would get their long-awaited grandchild, she never quite knew what to say.

Little did Dilara know that Events were conspiring in her favor. She could not see that in her home district of Kadikoy a tiny mouse was crouching in its hole across the street from her apartment. She could not hear the rumble of the truck that, several hours from now, would cause a loose brick to fall from a neighboring building, which would scare the mouse from its hole, which would frighten the spice peddler's donkey into knocking over his cart, sending a billow of jasmine tea up into the air. And Dilara could not feel the gust of wind, currently on its way across the desert sands, that would gather that billow and send it cascading up into the window above, where it might awaken her from her afternoon nap and send her outside to see what all the fuss was about.

All across The World, Chains such as these were constantly in motion—the stratagems of multiple departments working hand-in-hand with Case Workers in the Big Building. But one by one, they were slowly unraveling, for each had a weak link within their structure: Sleep . . . that knits up the raveled sleeve of care.

Thus, as Dilara Saffet boarded the bus and headed back to her apartment for lunch and some much needed rest, the chances that she would come outside and "accidentally" bump into Ati the postman were slowly slipping away.

Gandan Monastery, Sühbaatar Province, Outer Mongolia

"Anybody awake?"

The incomparable Li Po stepped up to the top of the bell tower, reading the text message that had just flashed across his Blinker. Down below, the youngest members of the Order practiced their forms and prostrations, completely unaware of the crisis that continued to mount.

"Isn't every 1?" he typed back.

With his shaved head and traditional garb, Po may have resembled the countless others who frequented this sanctuary, but he possessed a secret that only thirty-six others shared: though his chosen homeland wouldn't feel the brunt of the Glitch in Sleep for several more hours, if the situation in The Seems was not brought under control, a Ripple Effect could turn the countryside to chaos.

"R things as bad there as r here?" came the reply over Fixer-Chat[21]. It was the Octogenarian (username: 80something) from her home in South Africa.

"Not yet," texted Numerouno, communicating in the only way his Vow of Silence allowed. *"But will b soon."*

"Told u this was mistake," a third username popped into the conversation—"Øhands"—aka No-Hands Phil. *"Not job 4 kids."*

"Not fair," defended the Octogenarian.

---

21. The private communications channel accessible only by active members of the Duty Roster.

"Truth hurts."

Po leaned against a crumbling statue, forever amused by his comrade's trademark "gruffness." Po also knew that Phil had enjoyed being "the new kid on the block," and perhaps his judgment was clouded by a slightly bruised ego.

"What was your score on the Practical, #36?" typed Fixer Po, waiting for a reply that he knew would never come. *"What was #37's?"*

Fixer #1 smiled, certain that No-Hands Phil was stewing in his own juices somewhere in the Caribbean, or wherever his boat was moored. But he couldn't deny that he too had reservations. Though Becker Drane had briefed for him on two separate occasions and always impressed with both his talent and his heart, the rumblings of Po's 7th Sense were truly starting to scare him.

"Give kid chance," intervened the Octogenarian. *"He'll get job don. : -)"*

Li Po was about to agree with her when Phil beat him to the punch.

"He bettr."

30 Custer Drive, Caledon, Ontario

Half a world away, Anna and Steven Kaley nervously paced around their bright new living room. Though they had been there for over a month, boxes were still half unpacked and painters' tape lay in bundles on the hardwood floors.

"What do you think we should do?" asked Anna. A glass of

Sleepytyme Tea was in her hand, but she was too upset to drink it.

"It'll pass." Her husband tried to comfort her. "This always happens to the new kid in town."

"But I think it's worse than we know. She's covering things up, just so we won't worry."

Steven leaned over and gave his wife a hug. The job in Toronto had seemed like the opportunity of a lifetime, and though he felt bad about uprooting his family, he had hoped for an easier transition.

"She's a tough kid, honey. She'll make it through—"

He stopped in midsentence as the door to the upstairs bedroom swung open and Jennifer came bounding down the stairs.

"Hey . . . have either of you guys seen my silver necklace?"

Jennifer was wearing sweatpants and an extra-large T-shirt—her typical nighttime attire—but she didn't seem to be tired at all.

"Aren't you supposed to be asleep, young lady?"

"I'm supposed to have traveled the world, but that hasn't happened yet either."

"Ha ha," jibed her dad. "Have you checked in your jewelry box?"

"I would if I could find it."

"Honey, I think it must be out in the garage," suggested her mom.

Jennifer rolled her eyes at her parents' lack of organizational skills, then went out back to take a look. The garage was a disaster area, with boxes stacked from ceiling to floor. One after another she sorted through the crates, and finally found her jewelry box amid the rubble, but there was no sign of her favorite necklace. She did, however, find something else that brought a smile to her face.

"Wow—I forgot about you."

The first two days of Jennifer's tenure at Gary Middle School hadn't been that bad. Sure, it wasn't easy to leave her friends behind and it was never fun to have the entire class turn and look at you when the teacher announced, "We have a new friend," but all in all, it seemed like a relatively cool place. Until the morning of the third day.

That was when the whispering started between two other girls in the hall about Jennifer's "dirty" blond hair and cut-off shorts and anklets that she wore. In Vancouver, this was cool as well as comfortable, but here, people seemed to think it was weird. Though she was certainly thick-skinned enough to take a little razzing, it quickly escalated to something much, much worse.

In the days that followed, the girls *and* the boys began to make fun of her, and even those kids who would not normally bully anyone did so just to fit in with the pack. Lies were spread about why she had left her old school, caricatures drawn on the wooden desks, and several times she was locked in the bathroom, just for fun. Through it all, no one besides the teachers came to her defense.

But that only added fuel to the fire.

Jennifer climbed back onto her bed and opened the little red binder that she had lifted from the box of books. Inside were all of her photos from back in Vancouver—everything from the black-cat cake with the M&M's eyes that she and her babysitter had baked one Halloween to a shot of her beloved Gram, from whom her mother said she'd gotten her "independence." Each turn of the page brought a smile to her face, until she found one loose photograph amid the plastic sleeves.

"Hi, you guys."

It was a picture of her and Solomon and Joely, standing in a field of dandelions at the edge of Johnson's Park.

"Life sucks here. How're you doing?"

Solly and Jo were the youngest of seven kids in the Peterson family, who had lived next door to the Kaleys before Jennifer was even born. When she first moved to Caledon, she had been on the phone with them nonstop, but as the days wore on, the calls had become more infrequent, and she couldn't help but get the feeling that they were starting to drift apart.

"That's cool. Tell everybody I said hi, okay?"

Jennifer tacked the picture up above her bed and tried to hold on to to the memories as best she could. On that day, they had played in a concrete pipe and pretended it was a submarine, drawing buttons and levers and controls in different colored chalk. But right now, that seemed like a long, long time ago.

She flipped off the light and crawled beneath the covers of her bed. For some reason she hadn't been able to sleep all night, but what did it matter anyway? When she woke up tomorrow it was going to be more of the same, if not worse.

Jennifer closed her eyes, laid her head down on the pillow, and for the first time since she moved from Vancouver to Caledon, the girl began to cry.

Your Worst Nightmare

Back on the Mission, Thibadeau's tip had led Becker and Simly to the one Bedroom in the department that every Tireless Worker tried to get themselves transferred to. And judging by the way Becker's 7th Sense was tingling, it felt like his old friend had steered him in the right direction.

"I've never been in the Dreamatorium before," noted Simly, looking up through the glass Transport Tube that served as a front door.

"Well, tonight's probably not gonna be your night."

Due to the sensitivity and privacy of people's dream lives, this was one of the most highly secure Bedrooms in Sleep. Unfortunately for Briefer Frye, it required a clearance level of eight-plus, but he was relegated to a six.

"But you can't go up there by yourself!" Simly was apoplectic.

If nothing else, Briefers were fiercely loyal to their Fixers and loathe to leave their side.

"Rules are Rules, my friend," answered Becker. "Trust me, I'd rather have you with me."

"You're a Fixer—use your priority override!"

"This is my first Mission, and I want to play it by the book."

"But they would never want you to face a Glitch on your own," implored the Briefer. "Especially after what happened on the Big One.[22]"

"There's no time for an argument right now. Dawn's gonna be here in"—Becker checked his Time Piece—"three and a half hours."

"But—but—" Simly could barely get the words out.

"This conversation is over. I've made my decision."

Becker felt bad about taking a hard line, but no matter how fond he was of his sidekick, he had to keep his professional distance.

"Fine." Simly took it hard as Becker swiped the graphite pad with his Badge. An automated voice replied:

"Clearance level nine. Access granted."

On that note, a suction sound began to build inside the tube and Becker pulled down his Transport Goggles and stepped beneath it.

"While I'm gone, get on the horn and find out anything you can about the Not-So-Great Depression. I think your source might have been on to something."

---

22. Fixer Fresno Bob Herlihy was mortally wounded when he tried to Fix a Glitch by himself, inadvertently triggering a devastating earthquake in Sector 81 (San Francisco, USA) in 1906.

"Yes, sir!" Simly perked up. "I'll call the Librarian at the IFR and have her Blink me the Mission Report ASAP."

"And keep your head up, Frye. Just because you're not going up doesn't mean I won't need you."

Simly saluted with newfound pride.

"See you on the Flip Side, sir."

Becker felt the suction of the Transport Tube begin to pull at his shirt.

"On the Flip Side."

As Becker cruised through the curves of glass like chocolate milk through a twisty straw, he was all too aware that the sand was beginning to run out. Though The World contains twenty-four distinct Time Zones, The Seems only has one, and the arrival of Dawn initiates all Chains of Events scheduled to take place. But if Today didn't match up with Tomorrow, then the dreaded Ripple Effect would occur.

"*Prepare for Dreamatorium arrival,*" announced the computer.

To be honest, Becker wished he was a little more prepared. He'd been to this Bedroom once before during Training, but it was more of a tour than a nuts-and-bolts education.

"*Dreamatorium arrival in 3 . . . 2 . . . 1 . . .*"

The moment the Fixer popped from the Transport Tube—"Whoa"—he found himself surrounded by bubbles—purple and glistening and floating through the air—except these bubbles were the size of basketballs. The Bedroom itself seemed built to accommodate them, for the walls were reinforced with pillows and there was not a sharp edge in sight. Becker was about to break out his Manual and do some further research, when—

"Tally ho!"

His head snapped around at the sound of a muffled shout. The voice had obviously come from inside the room, but no Tireless Workers were in sight.

"Higher, higher!" There it was again, louder this time. "They'll never suspect an aerial assault!"

It took Becker a moment to realize that the voice he was hearing was not coming from his radio or from anywhere else in the room, but from *inside* one of the bubbles. A closer inspection of the one nearest to his head revealed the source of all the noise.

A young boy no more than seven sat astride the saddle of a giant bird, flying through the sky toward a shimmering city of glass. In his hand was a scimitar, and behind him, an army of warriors on winged steeds of their own.

"Come, boys! We'll show these scoundrels who was meant to be the Ki—"

As the bubble was lost among its fellows, Becker quickly found that this was not an isolated phenomenon. Every single sphere in the room appeared to contain another world, utterly and completely unique from the rest . . . and that's when he remembered what these bubbles really were.

"Becker to Simly. Come in, Simly."

"Simly h . . . re. Wh . . . t's goi . . . g on up th . . . re?"

"This place is crawling with Dreams!"

That was no exaggeration. There was one with an old man inside, staring into a bathroom mirror at the visage of his younger self, who shook his head sadly. A chocolate Lab rolled about in an endless field of grass, with all the rawhide chew toys it could ever want. And a teenaged girl stood at home plate in a packed Yankee Stadium, with two outs and the bases full and the chance to etch her name into World Series lore.

Not all of the Dreams were fantastical, though. Many of them featured mundane scenarios such as people chatting or waiting for the bus, while others were so bizarrely constructed as to be indescribable. All of them floated aimlessly, like they had no dreamers to dream them.

"I got a bad feeling about this, Brief. None of them are being sent to Central Shipping at all."

"... can't ... hear ... y ... bre ... ing up ..."

The transmission was garbled, which was not unexpected, given the pillow-reinforced walls.

"Affirmative. Let me see if I can find better reception."

Becker put his Receiver back on the hook. It was bad enough that he had lost touch with his Briefer, but now his temples hurt and he felt a closeness in his throat. There was no other explanation for it—the Glitch was in this room and he now faced the prospect of Fixing it all by his lonesome.

To be fair, Becker considered calling in for backup. There were still a handful of active Fixers who had been a part of Clean Sweep and would have been more than happy to Leap into The Seems and lend their expertise. But he was a rookie, desperate to make his mark, and sometimes Pride can be your worst enemy.

So he rolled up his sleeves and decided to go it alone.

"C'mon, baby. Come to papa . . ."

Down on the floor below, Simly had downloaded the Mission Report from the IFR Library and was now hard at work reassembling the Glitchometer.

"Mamma Frye's pride and joy needs himself a Special Commendation."

He tentatively flipped the repaired switch and the needle bounced into action, focusing itself back on zero.

"Yeah, baby . . . that's what I'm talkin' about!"

But just as the device was starting to hum, black smoke churned out the sides again, along with a stream of green fluid.

"Slamnit!"

The Briefer chucked the machine aside, utterly dejected. In the history of the IFR, only two Seemsians had ever been promoted to Fixer,[23] and either Simly had to do something splashy soon or he would be doomed to the path of the Fryes who came before him—professional Brieferhood (totally respectable, yet short on glory) or accepting a desk job at Central Command.

"Concentrate, Simly. Imagine you're from The World."

With eyes closed so tight that steam was almost coming out of his ears, Simly tried to do what Becker had suggested earlier. He pretended he was a schoolboy from Amsterdam or São Paulo (places he had always wanted to visit but never had the chance) and sought to isolate the feeling that something had gone wrong in The Seems. But trying to locate his 7th Sense

---

23. Alannis Niboot and Al Penske (aka "the Toolmaster"), who was the inventor of most of the Tools in the current editions of the Catalog.

was like trying to use a muscle that you just didn't have, and facts were facts: Simly was born over here . . .

. . . and Fixers were born over there.

SHHH-KUH . . . BUBBA . . . GLUBBA . . . RATTA-TATTA . . . WHOOSH.

The machine that towered over Becker was a contraption unlike any other in The Seems. Well, that's not exactly true. The Wish Washer from the Department of Everything That Has No Department was also canister-fed, but instead of a blue detergent, this behemoth used a golden speckled fluid. Once that fluid left the canister, it was stream-fed through a web of filtration systems, combined with a cleansing agent, then carefully billow-blown through a four-pronged revolving wand, which churned out the world-containing bubbles one by precious one.

SHHH-KUH . . . BUBBA . . . GLUBBA . . . RATTA-TATTA . . . WHOOSH.

Becker didn't need to check his Manual to know that he was looking at the Dreamweaver, and judging by the veridical crispness of the worlds it was creating, it seemed to be in perfect working order.

"Simly, you there?" He whispered into his Receiver, but only static came across. At this point, Becker had little choice but to pry open the complex machine and try to locate the Glitch inside the cross-woven circuitry. But before he could reach into his Toolkit, something unexpected passed before his eyes.

It was a big black Dream bubble—or at least darker in shading—and the first of its kind that Becker had seen. There was still a world taking place, but it was different, less fun, and strangely enough, there was someone he recognized inside.

"Jennifer Kaley is a haley, and she has no friends!"

Becker was stunned to see Jennifer Kaley, the girl from Canada who had become his Mission Inside the Mission. She was on the playground of her school, encircled by a group of jeering kids.

"Leave me alone!" she begged.

"But Jenny . . . we love you!" said one of the girls, her voice dripping with sarcasm. "We're *so* happy you came to our school."

Jennifer tried to call for help from the teachers, who were busily chatting by the fence, but amid the cacophony of recess they didn't seem to notice what was going on.

"Why are you doing this to me?"

"Because it's fun!" said one of the boys, unrepentant. All the kids laughed and Jennifer tried to make a run at the side of the circle, but she was quickly pushed back into the center.

"Where you going?" asked another of the mob. "Don't you like us anymore?"

Helpless, Jennifer fought back tears, until someone from the crowd hurled a water balloon that struck her right in the face. She fell to her knees, where she buried her head in her hands and cried. But as the throng laughed even louder, none took note of something high above them in the sky . . .

Becker Drane's enormous face, hazy and distorted by the bubble's walls.

The Fixer didn't understand what he was looking at. He knew this had to be Jennifer Kaley's 532—the Dream that was supposed to make her feel better—but it didn't seem like it was going as Planned. Instead of brightening her hopes for tomorrow, this was going to destroy them altogether, and there was only one explanation for what was going wrong. He was too late, and the Glitch had already trashed the Dreamweaver, causing it to spew out mixed and mangled Dreams.

"Jennifer?" he tried to shout through the hazy membrane. "Can you hear me?"

Inside, there was no reaction, except more kids gathering around the awful spectacle.

The Rulebook was specific, especially where the Plan is concerned, and Becker knew he probably shouldn't get involved, but he couldn't just idly stand by and watch someone be tortured for no apparent reason. He didn't even know what he was trying to do—maybe Fix the Dream or at least disperse the crowd—but the moment his hand touched the surface of the bubble, it began to wobble and shake, and soon thereafter . . .

POP-WHAM!

When Becker recovered his bearings, he was immersed in total darkness. All he could hear was the falling of debris and static booming over his radio when he tried to reach his Briefer. He quickly shuffled through his Toolkit and found his Night Shades™, so he could get a better look at his surroundings.

Wherever he was, it certainly wasn't the Dreamatorium anymore. The explosion had sent him back through the wall of that chamber and into one of the sealed-off rooms he'd seen on the Sleep Foreman's blueprints. Through the infrared lenses, it looked to be an abandoned laboratory, filled with dusty test tubes, beakers, and canisters of the same make and model as those that fit into the Dreamweaver.

He brushed himself off and approached the cobwebbed walls, still trying to figure out where his Mission had taken him. On the outside of the old canisters were peeling white labels, inscribed with arcane symbols that he couldn't quite decipher. Good thing for Becker that Night Shades came with a language filter, and he flipped through the settings—"Gaelic," "Toltec," "Aramaic," "Obbinglobbish"—until he found the one he was looking for:

"Olde Seemsian."

The labels instantly translated, and Becker could now read what they said:

MONSTER IN THE CLOSET
LATE FOR THE FINAL EXAM AND FORGOT TO STUDY
THE BOTTOMLESS PIT

All in a rush, a wave of panic flooded his brain. He tried to make a run for it, because he knew whose territory he'd unwittingly stumbled upon, but an awful sound froze him in his tracks.

Giggling . . . evil and full of malicious glee.

"C'mon, Becker. Get yourself outta here."

He sprinted again, but the pathway back was blocked with wreckage from the explosion and the lab seemed to have no exit at all. Suddenly, the lights flipped on.

"Well, well, well. What do we have here?"

There were three of them, each wearing lab technician's coats that bore the insignia of the single closed eye. This meant they were officially Tireless Workers, but their teeth were rotted, their skin was pasty, and their eyes were swollen from toiling in the dark.

"Such a fine specimen . . ."

"So young . . . so tender . . ."

The technicians poked him like a melon.

"Get your hands off me," said Becker.

Ever since he was a young boy, Becker's mom had given him the same admonition right before she turned off the lights. A warning that she thought meant nothing—without realizing that many of the sayings of our World come from obscure corners of The Seems. He now found himself face-to-face with the origins of one of those sayings, a pack of mad geniuses whose specialty was designing the most horrible Dreams imaginable, "affectionately" known as . . .

The Bed Bugs.

"I sent in a request for a Taster," croaked the largest of the trio. "But I never thought he'd come."

"It's about time. They wonder why Nightmares aren't scary anymore, then they cut our budget like we're second-class citizens."

"I told you we should have gone on strike."

Becker tried to talk his way out of it.

"Listen, guys—great to see you and all, but I'm not the Taster you're looking for. I'm a Fixer on a Mission to find a Glitch." The Bed Bugs looked at each other, confused, as if they had never heard any of those terms. "I just hit a minor snag in my search, so if we're all done here—"

"I love the way he makes up stories!" said the one with the sweaty shirt. "Such imagination!"

"That should lend itself to a high degree of terror!"

"Maybe we should test the new batch on him!"

They burst into laughter and began scurrying about, collecting a series of instruments: a butterfly net, a ball of twine, a set of metal prongs.

"Seriously, you guys. This is a big mistake. I know you have a job to do, but I have to warn you, I'm trained in the art of Fixing, and nothing, I mean *nothing*, can compromise my Mission."

From out of his Toolkit, Becker pulled out his Sticks & Stones™ and was about to kick some serious butt, when he felt something sharp bite him right in his own. Becker turned to see a fourth Bed Bug, this one short and pimply and bearing a hypodermic needle—which had just been emptied into the Fixer's rump.

"Don't worry. Our last Taster totally recovered."

They all laughed again but the bad medicine had already found its way into Becker's bloodstream. The walls became woozy and the crooked shelves even more warped, and the Bed Bugs themselves began to change shape, morphing into horrifically tall insectosoid beasts.

"Well, he almost did . . ."

Following the sound of the explosion, Simly had radioed Central Command, but he wasn't getting the answer he was hoping for.

"With all due respect, Mr. Dispatcher, sir, the Manual is quite clear on this matter." The force of the bubble's detonation had knocked a stack of pillow tiles off the ceiling, but Simly had cleared a space beneath the Transport Tube. "Appendix B, Paragraph 6, Line 4: 'In a crisis situation, or if the assigned Fixer is rendered incapable, a Briefer *may* be granted a temporary elevation in clearance.'"

"*I repeat,*" said the Dispatcher, as humorless as ever, "*clearance denied.*"

"But sir, it's an emergency! I've been out of radio contact for—"

"*Are you requesting backup, Briefer Frye?*"

Simly was about to say, "Of course I want some backup, you stupid jarhead," but he bit his tongue. To call in an emergency team on Becker's first Mission would be a huge embarrassment to the Fixer, and regardless of the circumstances, it would forever plant a subconscious blemish on his record.

"Negative, sir."

"*Then carry on. Central Command out.*"

Simly slammed down his Receiver, then looked back up at the tube above. He was paralyzed between his respect for the Rules and his responsibility to his Fixer.

"Where the heck are you, Becker?"

The light in the walk-in freezer automatically turned on when the door opened, and in came the leader of the Bed Bugs.

"Where is it? Where is it?" Frost filled the air, and there were racks of canisters on the metal-grated shelves. But these containers had much more modern packaging than those in the other room. "Marty! Where's Today's Horrors?"

"Check on the back shelf," came the voice of the pimply one.

On the shelf in the back, shrink-wrapped and labeled in Seemsian Modern font (22 point), was a rack called:

TODAY'S HORRORS: A NEW SERIES OF NIGHTMARES FROM THE DEPARTMENT OF SLEEP

The vials had names like EXISTENTIAL ANGST, DIRTY BOMB, and YOU GO TO THE DOCTOR FOR A ROUTINE CHECKUP AND HE FINDS THIS STRANGE "GROWTH" ON YOUR BODY AND IT'S REALLY ITCHY AND RED AND GETS BIGGER AND BIGGER AND BIGGER UNTIL . . . But separate from the others was one with a skull and crossbones tag.

"Ahhh . . . there you are, my pretty."

It was labeled:

YOUR WORST NIGHTMARE (BETA)

Becker was still dazed and confused from the sedative but he was aware enough to tell that his situation wasn't good. He was strapped into an old metal chair, his arms affixed by leather cords, and the Bed Bugs were placing a conductive leather helmet on his skull.

"What are you doing to me?"

"The only way to measure the fear factor of our Nightmares is to test them on the Scaredy Cat."

Becker blanched, for he'd thought this primitive method of gauging abject horror had been banned long ago. Ever since the concept of Dreaming had been introduced, the notion of Nightmares had been fiercely debated. The decision had been made to grant the Bed Bugs autonomy to conduct a limited amount of "necessary evil." After all, a little helping of Fear is sometimes just what the doctor ordered.

"Is he all strapped in?" The lead Bed Bug returned, holding the canister with his metal tongs. Inside was a fluorescent yellow liquid, and a noxious mist floated from the top.

"Seymour, no! That one's still in development!"

"But how often do we get a specimen from the other side, right here in our own lab?"

Marty, the pimply Bed Bug, looked deeply concerned.

"But what if he doesn't come back? What if he's . . . scared to death?"

"Then we'll know it works!"

All of their reservations evaporated as they suddenly grasped the genius of Seymour's plan. The Bed Bugs burst into a new round of cackling and back-patting, as if on the verge of a great discovery.

"You're gonna be sorry for this," threatened Becker, finally starting to come around.

"That makes two of us!"

The Fixer struggled mightily, trying to free himself from the confines of the chair, but the leather straps dug into his skin. Behind him, the needle on the Scaredy Cat moved up the meter from "Mildly Disturbed" to "Anxiety Attack" to "I'm Totally Freaking Out, Man!" And there were many more settings still to go.

145

"Hold him down!"

While two Bed Bugs restrained his head, Marty jammed a funnel into Becker's mouth, and Seymour slowly poured "Your Worst Nightmare" straight down his throat.

"Sweet dreams, kid."

Ripple Effect

When Becker awoke, it was four hours later and the Bed Bugs were nowhere to be found. He was still strapped into the Scaredy Cat and the needle had reached "White Knuckles," which was only one setting down from the highest possible level of fear. Luckily, Becker didn't remember much from his Nightmare—he rarely recalled his Dreams—but the evidence that something bad had happened was indisputable. His wrists were marked with deep strap burns, his shirt soaked with sweat, and his body sore from exhaustion, like he'd just climbed a mountain the day before.

"Hello? Is anybody there?"

From somewhere deep in the recesses of the lab, it sounded like a party was going on. There was music, laughter, the clinking of champagne glasses, but Becker's invitation must have been lost in the mail.

"You got what you wanted! Now I have to get back to my Mission!"

The Bed Bugs must have been celebrating the success of their experiment, but in their jubilation they had neglected to double-check Becker's restraints. The leather on his right wrist had come a little bit loose—just loose enough for him to reach under his shirtsleeve and pull out his Finger Nail™.

It was a silly Tool and many Fixers mocked it as something MacGyver might use, but Becker liked MacGyver because he always got out of a jam. As he frantically cut himself loose, his mind raced with worst-case scenarios. Four hours was an eternity to be out of action, and Dawn must've already come and gone. By the time Becker sawed his way through the final strap, the pit in his stomach had turned into a chasm.

"Becker to Simly! Simly, come in."

Still nothing but static.

"Fixer #37 to Central Command, come in. Over!"

Nothing.

Nothing at all.

Back in the Dreamatorium, Becker began to see that things were even worse than he had feared. There were no more bubbles floating through the air, just the evidence of soapy liquid on the floor where they had popped. He knew this was the result of the Dream he had unintentionally exploded, and to make matters worse, the machine that produced them had gone into shutdown.

"*Prepare for Dreamatorium departure,*" announced the voice of the computer as Becker stood above the Transport Tube. He needed to reconnect with his Briefer. He needed to talk to his superiors. And more than anything else, he needed to get the Mission back online. *"Dreamatorium departure in 3 . . . 2 . . ."*

When Becker's feet hit the ground, he grabbed for his Receiver, but he was rudely interrupted by the screeching of his Blinker.

194 MISSED CALLS

Uh-oh. Someone had been trying to reach him for quite some time—a lot of someones—and judging by the red flag next to each communication, he wasn't sure he wanted to hear what they had to say. He was about to suck it up and listen to the first one when he heard the sound of someone sobbing amid a pile of fallen pillowstones.

"Simly? Is that you?"

His Briefer didn't look up, his head tucked between his knees.

"Simly! What's wrong?"

"I'm sorry, sir. I didn't know what to do." Simly's voice was cracking and his eyes were red from crying. "They wouldn't give me clearance to go in."

"Just calm down and tell me what happened."

Simly stood up and tried to dust himself off, but Becker could tell he was barely holding it together.

"When we lost contact, I tried to get a priority override, but they wouldn't give it to me. So after an hour, I had to call in for a backup team. I'm sorry, Becker, I didn't want to do that to you."

"Don't worry, Sim. You did the right thing."

"It didn't matter, though." The Briefer was tearing at his hair. "No backup teams were available!"

"What do you mean no backup teams were—?"

"By that time, the Glitch had left Sleep and infiltrated three other departments! It was moving so fast, nobody could even figure out where to start! You don't know what's happening over there, man. You just don't know . . ."

The enormity of the disaster came crashing down upon the Briefer's shoulders and he fell back to the ground in tears.

"What happened up there, Becker?" He wept. "Where were you?"

Night Watchmen's Station, Department of Sleep, The Seems

RIPPLE EFFECT! RIPPLE EFFECT!

When Becker returned to the Night Watchmen's station, he expected to see a bundle of activity, but all he found was the cavernous room, illuminated by red emergency lights and only a Skeleton Crew on duty. On each of their screens, the same awful message flashed again and again and again:

RIPPLE EFFECT! RIPPLE EFFECT! RIPPLE EFFECT!

Most of the Night Watchmen were staring numbly at their Windows, while over by the craft service table, NW #42 was weeping onto the shoulder of his supervisor.

"Can someone please tell me where I can find Night Watchman #1?" Becker asked.

A group of exhausted employees heard him, but instead of the instant respect he was granted upon first entrance, something else was in their eyes: a mixture of rage, contempt, and shock at what was taking place in The World they loved. And from the way they simply turned away, it was pretty obvious who they held responsible.

Becker swallowed hard and scanned about for the Watchman who had helped him earlier, and found him still at his post—glued to the screen with his headset dangling uselessly around his neck.

"You're too late." The way he looked straight ahead, Becker felt like an invisible man.

"Wasn't anyone able to Fix it?"

"Po and Philadelphia neutralized the Glitch, but the Chains of Events had already slipped too far! Nature went off-line first, then Weather, and from there it was like a snowball. The Plan was in shambles and before you knew it, Reality itself started to lose integrity . . ."

"But surely the Powers That Be—"

"There's nothing they can do! Don't you understand?" His voice dropped to a whisper of terrible defeat. "There's nothing . . ."

Night Watchman #1 rose from the chair, handed Becker his headset, and slowly walked away.

"Take a look for yourself."

Becker attached the headphones and stared at the monitor, and when he saw what was taking place in sector after sector, he couldn't believe his eyes.

In Bangladesh, the monsoon rains were made of nails instead of water.

In Rejkovic, the temperature had reached 243 degrees.

And in Mexico City, Gravity had lost its hold, and everything that wasn't tied down was sailing off into the sky. People were screaming and trying to hold on for dear life, and the wild fear in their eyes betrayed the unfathomable experience of being trapped inside a World gone mad.

The same numbness that affected the others began to settle over Becker. How could he have let this happen? His fingers mechanically found their way to the keyboard and punched in the numbers for Sector 33, Grid 514.

"Oh, no."

Highland Park, New Jersey, USA

As soon as Becker stepped back through the Door, he dropped his Toolkit and ripped off his Badge and pedaled frantically back to 12 Grant Avenue. He was no longer a Fixer (for there was nothing left to Fix), but simply the son of Dr. and Dr. F. B. Drane, and the older brother to a little boy named Benjamin. And he was more scared than he'd ever been in his life.

While Becker pumped his feet as fast as they would go, cars and people were headed in the opposite direction, desperately trying to get out of town. But little did they know, there was no safe haven left. Bark was literally melting off the trees, while high above in the sky, the moon had cracked itself in two.

"Becker—you're going the wrong way!" Dr. Kole was running by in his bathrobe, clutching a sack spilling over with his beloved books. "We have to get to higher ground!"

Becker wanted to stop and tell him that somehow this would

all be okay, but he knew in his heart that it wouldn't, so he sped on past without saying a word.

"Mom, Dad!"

Much like he'd done the day before, Becker dropped his bike on the lawn and flew inside the house. On the couch in the living room, his father was clutching Benjamin, who was crying like a baby, while his mother stared at him in disbelief.

"Becker, but—I don't understand."

"Mom, I tried. I swear, I tried the best I could. But the Bed Bugs, they knocked me out, and the Glitch—" As he stammered out an explanation, Becker had the distinct recollection of the time when he'd broken his mom's favorite sunglasses, which he'd borrowed without asking. But unlike then, when she had reassured him "it's no big deal, sweetheart," no such relief was coming.

"How is this possible?" she said. "Who are you?"

"What are you talking about? I'm me!"

His parents looked at each other, utterly confused, just as Becker's spitting image came scrambling from the kitchen. In the Me-2's hands were a ration of canned goods, and it looked just as surprised to see Becker as Becker was to see it.

"What the heck are you doing here?" said the Me-2. "Why aren't you Fixing the Glitch?"

"Because the Glitch can't be Fixed!"

The Me-2 was about to ask why, when—

"Will somebody please tell me what on earth is going on around here!" shouted Professor Drane, as Benjamin's wails increased to an ear-splitting shriek.

"I'll explain everything later, but right now we have to—"

Both Becker and the Me-2 stopped talking, because they

were saying the exact same thing at the exact same time (in the exact same voice).

"Shut up, Me! I'll handle this!"

"Like you handled the Glitch? No thank you!"

Becker started to respond with anger, but he realized the Me-2 was right. He'd blown the Mission and cost The World dearly.

"I—I—"

Enraged, the Me-2 lunged at Becker and grabbed him around the throat. While they wrestled on the floor, his mom began to scream, matched only by the cries of horror that filtered in through the window.

"You've doomed us all, you incompetent fool!"

Becker was still struggling to take a breath when his hand finally found the dial on the back of the Me-2's neck. He flicked it to "Off," and instantly the doppelganger began to deflate—but not without a parting shot.

"This . . . is . . . all . . . your . . . faul—"

The Me-2's voice eked to a halt.

Becker rose to his feet, but any solace he may have felt from the end of the fight was quickly wiped away by the sight of his mom fainting to the floor.

"Becker, please, what's happening?"

"There's no time to explain, Dad! We've got to get out of here!"

Becker figured if he could just get his family back to the Door, he might be able to take them to the safety of The Seems before it was too late. But suddenly, from outside his house, there was a terrible ripping sound, followed soon after by a blinding blue light—and Becker didn't even need to look to know what it meant. He did anyway, though, and there it was: the Fabric of Reality, tearing like a piece of cloth through the middle of his neighborhood, to expose the In-Between behind it.

And as the ground beneath his feet began to rupture and shake, it hit Becker Drane like a ton of bricks. He knew exactly who was to blame for the end of The World. He was.

"Marty, you nincompoop!"

Laboratory of the Bed Bugs, Department of Sleep, The Seems

Seymour the Bed Bug was fuming.

"What's it gonna take for you to mix a real Nightmare?"

Marty was crushed. Though the beta test for **YOUR WORST NIGHTMARE** had gone swimmingly (judging by the gesticulations of the unconscious Taster in the chair), the Scaredy Cat said otherwise.

"But it made it to 'White Knuckles' . . ."

"White Knuckles! If I wanted White Knuckles, I'd take **MONSTER IN THE CLOSET** for the thirty-fourth time!"

Marty and the other Bed Bugs in the room dropped their heads in shame.

"You heard what the VP said—'If you don't deliver me a Nightmare that makes it to "Curled Up in the Fetal Position and Crying for Mommy," you're out and I'm bringing in Hubie's team.' "

"Hubie?" cried the sweaty-shirted Dr. Glorp. "Hubie couldn't mix a Nightmare if it hit him on the head!"

"Don't you think I know that?" Seymour threw an empty beaker at his colleague, which shattered on the wall. "Now go get me **OLD FAITHFUL** before this imbecile wakes up!"

In the chair before them, Becker Drane had finally started to stir. It had been a horrible Dream, worthy of its name, and he was still not free from its devastating spell.

"It's not my fault . . . Mom, Dad . . . we have to get to the . . . Benjamin . . ."

"Don't worry, munchkin. I'm going to take you far, far away from all this." Seymour chuckled and leaned in to the semiconscious Fixer. "To someplace much, much worse."

Just then, Glorp returned with a dusty old decanter.

"I don't understand, Seymour. I thought we had retired **OLD FAITHFUL.**"

"I'm sick of these new-agey Nightmares. The classics are the classics for a reason!" Seymour dangled the last remaining milliliter of **YOUR WORST NIGHTMARE** over the crusty container. "And with one drop of this . . ."

The instant the two Nightmares combined, the liquid began to bubble and froth.

". . . what's old becomes new!"

Seymour raised the vial over his head, triumphant, and his partners roared with delight.

"Someone call an exterminator?"

The Bed Bugs whirled around to see a tall, lanky Seemsian come flying into the room. His body was draped from head to toe in Tools, and stamped on his chest was the block letter "B," which he wore as proudly as all the Briefers who were ever named Frye.

"Now get your hands off my Fixer," Simly demanded, "or else!"

The Bed Bugs stood stunned for a second before Seymour broke into a yellow-toothed grin.

"This it too good to be true! Two Tasters in one day."

The others grabbed their nets and prepared to seize their second victim, but Simly was more than ready. He pulled a thin (ozone-friendly) aerosol canister off his Utility Belt and sprayed it in their faces. The Bed Bugs immediately began to cough and choke and fall on the floor, writhing about in agony. Simly made sure to soak each one a second time, then unstrapped his dazed compatriot.

"Becker! Becker! Are you okay?"

A quick slap to the face seemed to bring the Fixer back to this reality.

"Simly! What's—what's happening?"

"I'm trying to get you out of here!"

"But the Ripple Effect . . . it's tearing The World apart!"

"It was just a bad dream, Becker. There hasn't been any Ripple Effect. At least not yet!"

Becker didn't believe him at first—it was all so fresh in his mind—but as the truth of Simly's words rang home, his mind and body filled with newfound strength. There was still time to do his job and do it right.

"Now hurry up, sir," said Simly, pulling free the last of the straps. "This stuff wears off after a couple minutes."

"What did you use on those guys?"

"Something my grandpa gave me when he found out I was going to Sleep."

He held up the can, which had a picture of a guy in a lab-coat inside a circle, with a red line through it.

"Bed Bug Repellent™!" shouted Seymour, dragging himself off the floor and gasping for air. "Very clever indeed."

"But not clever enough!" issued Marty, color flooding back into his face. In fact, all four Bed Bugs had started to shake off the effects. "That might have worked back in Milton Frye's day, but we've spent the last twenty years building up a resistance to his pathetic concoction!"

"Um . . ." Simly was at a loss for the first time that night. "I'm all out of ideas, boss."

Becker normally would have busted out his Speed Demons™ at a time like this, but in all the hurry of his first Mission, he'd left them in the closet right next to his Chuck Taylor's. With just his regular kicks on and the Bed Bugs blocking each and every exit, there was only one way left to go.

"Dude, put on your Concrete Galoshes™."

"Why? What's that gonna do?"

"Just do it."

Snorchestral Chamber, Department of Sleep, The Seems

Directly below the Chamber of Horrors, on the eighth floor of the department, was a packed auditorium, complete with band shell, red velvet seating, and balcony boxes for the Powers That Be. The same legendary ensemble had sold out the show every night since the beginning of Time, and tonight was no exception.

"Shhh!"

In the fourth row, the Snoozemaster shoved his way past several annoyed patrons to get to seats 4D and 4E.

"I am sorry, *mon cheri*, but zis Glitch . . ." The young Scent Designer who was his date for the evening didn't want to hear it. "You must understand, I had to rebuild ze Snooze from Scra—"

"Shhh!"

The rest of the second row didn't want to hear it either, for up onstage, the Snorchestra was entering into its climactic movement. Musicians were playing a host of odd instruments—pots and pans, kettle drums, a piece of wood being sawed—while a chorus of noseblowers laid down a harmony of phlegm. In the pit below, a conductor waved his baton, while technicians recorded every sound of the awful clamor onto pancake reels destined for Central Shipping.

"Wonderful! Wonderful!" exhorted the Snoozemaster, as a particularly horrible cacophony erupted from the stage. Fortunately for him and the rest of the audience, protective headphones were issued upon entrance, which translated the harsh snores into sweet and dulcet tones. "And 'ere comes ze finale."

The music swelled to a crescendo and the crowd began to rise to its feet, but before the Fat Lady could sing, a swarm of lab-coated freaks came crashing down from above.

"Bed Bugs!"

In a wave of panic, the concertgoers scattered for the doors, while the hapless scientists staggered to their feet. They had survived the fall unscathed but were now up against something that was far, far worse.

"No. Not the Snorchestra," cried Seymour, clutching his hands to his unprotected ears. "Make it stop. *Make it stop!*"

But the Snorchestra could not stop, for Snoring itself was

one of the oldest and most maddening sounds ever created, and the musicians who played it were devoted to its every note.

High above, Becker and Simly gently floated toward the ground. Only moments before, the combined weight of their Concrete Galoshes had caused the ancient floor of the Chamber of Horrors to collapse, sending all of its inhabitants plunging down below. Luckily, the Fixer and Briefer were far more prepared for a free-fall than the Bed Bugs—deploying their Chutes & Ladders™ and donning a pair of Earplugs™—but the successful stratagem did not come without a price.

"This isn't good, sir," said Simly, pointing to the chaos below.

"This is worse."

When Becker held up his Blinker, the Briefer knew he wasn't kidding, for the light was flashing red and a painfully simple text message was writing itself across the screen:

VIOLATION! FIXER #37 SUSPENDED
FROM DUTY! VIOLATION!

A Glimmer of Hope

The door to the office of the highest-ranking employee in Sleep was made of frosted glass and stenciled with the name of the man who worked inside:

DOMINIC DOZENSKI,
ADMINISTRATOR, DEPT. OF SLEEP

Behind that door was Dominic himself, with his walrus mustache, three-piece suit, and gold-plated pocketwatch (inscribed with the departmental insignia). He sat silently behind his messy desk, deliberately flipping through the pages of a thick, hardcover book while across from him, Becker and Simly reclined in two pleather Love Seats.

"Excuse me, sir, but—"

The Administrator silenced Becker with a single finger, which he then licked and used to turn another page. On the wall above them, the clock ticked forward and Becker wanted to say, "C'mon, dude, let's get this over with so I can get back to my Mission," but he was severely outranked and had no choice but to bite his tongue.

As Dominic made a note to himself in the margin, Becker let his eyes wander over the office. Sleep-related arcana littered the walls, while the bookshelves were filled with Seemsian best-sellers such as *The Unauthorized Miracle* and *Why Should They Have All the Fun?: How to Overcome Your Resentment and Learn to Love The World Again.* And prominently displayed on the wall behind the desk, just as it was in the office of all the other Administrators, was the famous painting known as *The Thirteenth Chair.*[24]

"Ahem."

Dominic cleared his throat and slammed the book shut. "Do you know what this book is, Fixer Drane?"

"It's the Rulebook, sir."

"That's right. It's the Rulebook—and do you know why we have a Rulebook?"

Becker was smart enough to know this was a rhetorical question, so he kept his mouth shut.

"Rules are the foundation of any good organization, son. For without Rules, even an organization as . . . organized as The Seems can go bad. Like an apple rotting to the core."

"I realize that, sir, but—"

"Don't interrupt me, son."

"Yes, sir."

---

24. This masterpiece, painted by the Original Artist, depicts the twelve founding members of the Powers That Be gathered around their conference table in the Big Building, with the chair at the head of the table conspicuously empty.

"When you and you and I took these jobs, we agreed to follow these Rules to the best of our ability. Even when it didn't seem like the right thing to do!"

Becker and Simly glanced at each other, not sure where this was going, while Dominic swiveled a monitor on his desk around to face them.

"Bad enough that your Briefer trashed the Chamber of Horrors without clearance . . ."

Onscreen, a closed-circuit security camera depicted Seymour's lab, still fumigated with Bed Bug Repellent.

"Bad enough you interrupted the Snorchestra in mid-performance!"

In the Snorchestral chamber, the Conductor was lambasting his Promoter, while Bed Bugs were being carried out on stretchers.

"And bad enough that the Glitch in Sleep has still not been Fixed!"

Back in Central Shipping, the pile of unmailed Good Night's Sleep had reached epic proportions.

"But most offensive of all"—Dominic slammed the Rulebook down on the desk and opened it to a clearly marked page—"You violated the Rule of Thumb!"

"What are you talking about?" retorted Becker, flabbergasted. "I did no such thing!"

"Oh really? Would you care for me to read it to you?"

Becker didn't, because he already knew what it said. Everyone did. The Rule of Thumb was the one Rule in The Seems that no one wanted to break.

"That won't be necessary, sir."

"Oh, I think it will be, young man. I think it will be."

Dominic picked up the book and began to read:

The Rule of Thumb: No employee of The Seems, present, past, or future, shall knowingly (or unknowingly) interfere with the well-being of any person, inhabitant, entity, or individual in The World, without the prior written consent of the Powers That Be. *Cicae luci combustem, periodi!*

Dominic sadly closed the book and his voice seemed to soften.

"In other words, you cannot run around playing with people's lives."

Becker quickly spun over everything that had happened that night, and in his heart of hearts he knew what Dominic was getting at.

"Do I need to spell it out for you?"

The Administrator banged on his keyboard and up came the Dreamatorium, empty save for a janitorial crew sent in to clean up the remains of the broken Dreams. A touch of a button, however, rewound the picture back to the moment when an explosion sent Becker through the wall, and further back still, to the point when he had first entered the room.

"Now, do you deny that this is you?"

"No," said Becker, tentatively. "But I don't see how—"

Dominic hit play, and the action slowly moved forward, to where Becker discovered a bubble that was darker than the rest. The one that contained a young girl who had grown up in Vancouver, British Columbia, but now lived in Caledon.

"And here is where you so brilliantly *destroyed* Dream #532—a rare and delicate piece of work."

"That was an accident. And besides"—Becker rose to his feet and pounded on the desk himself—"I thought Jennifer was supposed to get a Dream to make her feel better! A *special* Dream!"

"She was!"

"Well, it looked like a Nightmare to me! I had no choice but to go in there—"

"You're not given enough *information* to make that kind of decision!"

The two of them were only inches apart and Simly was afraid it might come to blows.

"If you were doing your job instead of trying to be a hero, then you would have trusted in the Plan . . ." Dominic slapped the space bar on his keyboard, accessing the Dream database. "And you would have had patience to wait for the rest of the 532."

Onscreen, Jennifer Kaley was once again surrounded by the hounding crew of bullies. Her hair was still wet from the water balloon (and the tears) and it looked like there would be no end to her suffering. But then something strange happened: the crowd dispersed and a look of wonder slowly came over her face. Something (or someone) seemed to be approaching, and she could not believe her eyes . . .

"Now here comes the good part," explained Dominic. But he and the video were interrupted by a knock on the door.

"Enter!"

One of the Tireless Workers poked his head inside.

"She's here, sir."

"Well, it's about time!"

As Dominic's assistant went to retrieve the new arrival, Becker felt himself begin to sweat. For the first time, he was starting to realize the magnitude of his violation.

"You rang?"

But when the door opened again, and Becker saw who walked in, he realized that he *hadn't* realized the magnitude of his violation at all.

"Is that . . . ," asked Simly, jaw on the floor.

"Yeah. That's her."

Judging by her bare feet and the saltwater in her hair, Fixer Casey Lake had just been yanked off a pretty tasty wave. And she didn't look happy about it.

"I came as soon as I could."

Casey threw a nod to Becker as if to say, "Hey, mate," and Becker nodded back, embarrassed that it had come to this.

"I'm sorry to have to call you in at this late hour," Dominic apologized. "But things have gotten completely out of hand."

"What seems to be the problem?"

"You tell me! I've got a Fixer with a Thumb Violation, a Briefer with a 318 . . ." Dominic pulled what looked like parking tickets off his desk. "And a Glitch without a Fixer wreaking havoc on the Plan!"

"Hey!" said Simly, without thinking. "Becker's done an awesome job toni—"

But Dominic shut him up with a glance.

"Time was a Fixer came in and took care of business—one, two, three."

"A Glitch is no easy matter, Administrator Dozenski." Casey thanked the Tireless Worker who brought her a towel, and she sat on the edge of Dominic's desk. "In fact, it's just about the trickiest bitzer in the book."

"That's why I need you to finish the job—because Junior here has botched the whole thing up!"

"You're speaking about a Fixer, sir," Casey's voice raised to a firmer pitch, "and you will speak of him with respect!"

Fixers and Briefers were a close-knit family, bound by the crucible of what they'd endured during Training. But Dominic was not impressed.

"I've spoken to everyone I need to—including Central Command—and I assure you, I will have this little boy's Badge."

The blood ran from Simly's face and Becker felt like he wanted to vomit. He knew the penalties for a Rule of Thumb Violation were severe, but he never considered that he might actually lose his job.

"The Court of Public Opinion will be hearing his case tomorrow, but in the meantime, Dawn is on her way, and if she gets here before it's too early, then we could be looking at a full-blown Ripple Effect!"

The very mention of the possibility sent a shiver through Becker, for he had just seen what Ripple Effects look like first-hand. And though Casey was ready to fight for her colleague through thick and thin (after all, she was the one who'd nominated him for his promotion in the first place), such a thing could not be allowed to happen.

"I'm sorry, mate. Maybe if I can Fix this quick, I can put in a good word."

This was almost worse than his Worst Nightmare, because at least that one he'd woken up from. His eyes fell to his Badge and the double-sided wrench that was stenciled onto it. With someone as powerful as Dominic lobbying against him, there was little doubt which way the Court would decide, and by this time tomorrow, the best job he could hope for would be Pencil Pusher. But more than likely he would just be sent back to The World to become a regular kid again.

"I'm sorry, Casey. I was only trying to help her."

"No worries, Drane." Lake gave him a reassuring nudge. "Everybody makes a blue of it sometimes."

Becker nodded dejectedly, then patted Simly on the shoulder, who was fighting to hold back tears. But as he picked up his Toolkit and ambled sadly toward the door, something popped into the Fixer's head. A Memory—only five weeks old—that had already become submerged in everything that had happened since. Perhaps this was the moment his old Instructor had been talking about.

Perhaps there was still a glimmer of hope.

Institute for Fixing & Repair, The Seems, Five Weeks Ago

On the grounds of the IFR there was a small tented pavilion where lectures, weddings, and symposiums were occasionally held. Today's event was the Elevation Ceremony of one F. Becker Drane, a Briefer who had distinguished himself on seventeen challenging Missions, but particularly on his most recent assignment to the Department of Weather.

The entire Fixer and Briefer corps were sporting their dress blues, while higherups from the Big Building sipped cocktails and ate "pigs in a blanket" in the late summer air. Over by the punch bowl, Becker tried to steal a moment for himself, for even though it was fun to be the center of attention for a little while, the endless schmoozing, handshakes, and pats on the back had started to become a little much.

"Worth its weight in gold, huh?"

Fixer Blaque caught Becker admiring his shiny new Badge.

"More."

The Instructor walked up beside him. With his formal attire and blue-tinted shades glinting in the sun, he was that much more impressive.

"Can I borrow you for a minute?"

"Of course, sir."

They took their plastic cups and strolled across the lawn toward Finnegan's Pond.[25]

"Is there something wrong, sir?"

"Not at all, Cand—I mean, Fixer Drane. There's just something I wanted to show you."

Halfway there, they crossed paths with Briefers Carmichael and Von Schroëder.

"We right on your heels, yo."

"Ja, dogg. *Wir sind* right on your heelz."

"*Wunderbar!*" Becker laughed as C-Note and Frau Von Schroëder bumped fists. "I guess I'll see you on the Flip Side."

"On the Flip Side," they replied in unison.

Fixer Blaque smiled, then led Becker down toward the gazebo by the water's edge. "It's good to have friends—especially on a job like this."

---

25. Named after Michael Finnegan, the inventor of salt-free water for lakes, streams, and ponds.

"Yes, sir."

The gazebo itself was painted white and Blaque pointed to the gold-plated dedication that was inscribed above the stairs:

Dedicated to the Memory of Fixer Tom Jackal
Lost in Time, 13,444
All Gave Some. Some Gave All.

"Tom was my best friend. Did you know that?"

"No, sir."

"He was a good man, and the best Fixer I ever met. Even though I know he's in a Better Place, I miss him terribly."

A breeze blew in and light sparkled off the pond, and Becker could tell that Fixer Blaque had something to get off his chest, so he remained silent.

"The last Mission we ever went on together was called 'Hope Springs Eternal.'"

Becker had never heard of that one but he was all ears. For him, hearing about legendary Missions was almost as good as going on them.

"Back then, The World was full of despair, and everything they tried to do here in The Seems had failed to fix the problem. So a decision was made to send a group of Fixers to the Middle of Nowhere, in order to bring back some Hope."

"I thought the Middle of Nowhere was off-limits."

"It is."

Fixer Blaque took another sip of punch, then continued.

"Three of us were chosen—me, Tom, and Lisa Simms, who I think you've served with before."

"Yes, sir. On the 'Broken Heartstring.'"

"Anyhow, we took the Train out to the End of the Line, and believe me, nothing can prepare you for what it's like. Time, Nature, Reality—they don't exist out there—it's just an endless wasteland full of Nothing."

Becker could only imagine what that looked like, because the only people who had ever seen the Middle of Nowhere didn't come back. This must have been the story behind the picture on Blaque's "Wall of Fame."

"Tom and Lisa took the mountains, I took the dead riverbed, and for eighteen days we searched to no avail. But at sunset on the nineteenth day, I spotted something—a cave, with a strange flickering light inside of it. I probably should have waited for help, but there was no signal on my Receiver and not much time. So I went in on my own."

The way Blaque's massive fingers were gripping the railing of the gazebo, it was like he was back inside that cave again.

"I wish I could describe it to you. Hope, flowing like water from a spring in the rock—and so bright that I could barely stand to be in its presence."

Becker thought he noticed his Instructor wincing at the memory of an old wound.

"Two jars I know I filled, but midway through the third I must have blacked out. The next thing I remember, Tom and Lisa were dragging me out of there. How they found me, I still have no idea—but we pulled it off. We brought back a little bit of Hope for The World."

"Cool."

Over by the ceremony, the crews had begun to break down the stands, and the crowd filtered back toward the monorail that would return them to their homes and jobs. The teacher watched them go for a time, before finally looking down at his student.

"You're one of the most talented Candidates I've seen at the IFR in a long, long time, Becker. Not just because of your skills and your 7th Sense but because of your dedication to the Mission. And make no mistake about it, you deserve to wear that Badge."

Becker felt his own rush of pride.

"But sometimes I forget you're only twelve years old."

"Yes, sir. Sometimes I do too."

The Instructor laughed heartily, a sound Becker always loved because it was so infectious. But it didn't last long, for now was the time he'd chosen to deliver his most precious gift.

"There comes a moment in the life of every Fixer when everything you've tried has failed, and there's nowhere left to turn—and trust me, it happens to us all—but when that moment comes for you, Becker, I want you to remember . . ."

Fixer Blaque reached into his pocket and pulled out a souvenir from the most dangerous Mission of his career.

"You'll always have *this*."

Office of the Administrator, Department of Sleep, The Seems

"Where in the name of the Plan did you get *that*?"

Even the great Casey Lake was blown away by the sight of what Becker was holding.

"Graduation present."

"Beats a Williams-Sonoma gift card."

"I'll say."

In the palm of Becker's hand was a small glass cube, with a tiny speckle of light inside it.

"What is it?" asked Simly.

"A Glimmer of Hope," answered Casey, as if she'd seen one before.

Becker had stashed it in the Secret Compartment of his Toolkit for a rainy day, like when he was on his twenty-fourth Mission, dangling from the Edge of Sanity. But he would never have a twenty-fourth (not to mention a second) without completing his first.

"It's . . . beautiful," Dominic marveled, briefly under the spell of the precious substance. "But this doesn't change anything! We've still got a Glitch in Sleep that needs to get Fixed!"

"Not for long," said Becker, newfound confidence beginning to build.

"It's too late for fancy footwork now, kid! You're off the job!" The Administrator reached out to yank Becker's Badge off his chest, but Casey slapped his hand away.

"Not so fast, mate. Unless I hear a better idea, this is the only chance we've got."

Dominic's face turned bright red, but taking on Casey Lake was a far different cry than challenging a rookie Fixer on his first assignment.

"Fine! But if the Ripple Effect hits, it's on your head, not mine!"

"So be it." Casey seemed to relish the opportunity. "It's your show now, Fixer Drane."

With all eyes on him, Becker placed the cube on Dominic's desk and tried to remember the instructions that Fixer Blaque had given him. He opened the small latch that kept the cover closed, and as if on cue, the tiny Glimmer gently rose into the air.

"Now, everybody clear your thoughts because we don't want to cross any signals."

The only way to activate a Glimmer of Hope is to hope for what you want with everything you've got, and if the thoughts are pure enough, it's almost certain to come true. The only problem, though, is that you can't fool Hope—you really have to *feel* it. So Becker looked back upon the Mission and called to heart everything that he was hoping for most that night.

"Do you need help hoping, sir?" asked Simly, thinking of *his* Mission Inside the Mission—the salesman in the Emmaus motel.

"No, dude. This one's on me."

Becker closed his eyes and began to hope for all that he was worth. He hoped for the woman in Turkey, that the Events conspiring in her favor would not be compromised, and that she would meet the lonely postman who was her perfect match. Then he hoped for Simly's hope—that Anatoly Svar would be able to make the drive home in time for his daughter's birthday.

"It's working!" shouted Simly, and sure enough the Glimmer rose higher and grew even larger. Becker's flow was almost interrupted by his Briefer's exuberance, but he managed to focus by hoping for Jennifer Kaley, that she would get her Dream after all, and that tomorrow would be a better day.

"What's going on?" cried Dominic, as exquisite white light filled the room.

"Cover your eyes!" shouted Casey, slapping on her own pair of Night Shades.

But Becker barely heard them, for he was shaking violently

and utterly transfixed by his last (but not least) hope: for some sign—a signal, a hint, a foreshadowing, a clue—that would lead them straight to the Glitch so that all of his other hopes could ultimately come true.

All at once, the light swelled to an unbearable brightness, and everyone in the room fell to the floor lest they be blinded by the possibilities of what might be.

There was a flash, a crack, and a **VWORPLE.** And when they opened their eyes, the Glimmer of Hope was gone.

But in its place was something else.

The Glitch in Sleep

At the Black Market, held on Saturdays and Sundays between nine and six, the erstwhile shopper can purchase virtually any substance manufactured in The Seems—from Epiphanies and Sighs of Relief to Last Straws and Pleasant Surprises—if they are willing to pay the price. But of all the commodities found on the portable tables and fold-up stands, few are harder to come by than Sleep.

Sitting on Dominic's desk, where the Glimmer of Hope had been, was a small amount of the precious dust. It was a light yellow, with the occasional silver sparkle, hermetically sealed inside a plastic sleeve. A single closed eye was stamped upon the face, indicating its authenticity, not to mention the location of manufacture.

"It can't be!" whispered Dominic, still blinking away the spots from his eyes. "The Master Bedroom is impregnable—even to a Glitch."

"Maybe it slipped in through one of the Refreshment Ducts," posited Becker.

"Too small," countered Casey. "But it could've come down through the Twinkler System."

"No way. No how." The Administrator became indignant. "I personally oversaw the construction of that entire room!"

"Then why don't you give them a call," Casey prodded.

"Fine! But this is a complete waste of Time."

As Dominic picked up the intercom, Simly lifted the packet of Sleep and stared at it closely. "I don't understand."

"The Glimmer's pointing to the one Bedroom I never thought the Glitch could penetrate." Becker tucked the empty case into his Toolkit for Posterity. "But then again, Hope never lies."

"This is Administrator Dozenski to Master Bedroom, Master Bedroom come in." Dominic listened for a response, but when he spoke again, it was without the same assurance. "Master Bedroom, please respond!"

The Administrator slowly lowered the Receiver.

"No answer."

That was all the confirmation Casey needed and she quickly seized command.

"I want a Level 5 lockdown through the entire department, four sets of Pajamas™, and Night Patrol placed on every conceivable way in or out of that room!"

"Done!" Dominic started scrambling to fill Casey's requests. "But if it's in the Master Bedroom, it may already be too—"

"You let us worry about that."

Becker grabbed his gear and readied himself for action. Though he was still technically going to Court tomorrow, he had much more important things on his mind.

"Now how do we get there?"

Decompression Chamber, Department of Sleep, The Seems

Up an ornate spiral staircase lay the entrance to the Master Bedroom, where the substance of Sleep was mixed and manufactured. But before entering, one must endure decompression,[26] for though the individual ingredients are essentially harmless, when combined, they produce an extremely intoxicating effect. Hence, all necessary precautions must be taken when risking exposure to the powerful compound.

"These don't look like pajamas," noted Simly as he stepped into the thick, protective suit. "They don't even have the little feets!"

"They're not supposed to," answered Dominic, pulling on his thick orange gloves. "Pajamas were designed to protect my Tireless Workers from the hazmats that lie beyond that door."

Simly gulped and buckled his boot one extra notch.

"Commence Sleep Decompression," said the computer, and a gauge on the wall dropped from yellow to orange. Becker and Casey were already geared up to the hilt and sifting through their Toolkits for the latest in Anti-Glitch technology. One by

---

26. Sleep can only be manufactured at under 16 hectopascals (6 millibars [8 kgf/cm^2]).

one they clicked on their extensions and removed the safeties, while Simly fiddled with his Briefcase.

"What do you guys think I should bring?"

"Just yourself, kid." Becker smiled, making an obvious reference to the classic Fixer Training film *Don't Be a Tool*, and Simly forced a grin. But the tension in the air was palpable.

"Sleep Decompression complete."

The light on the meter hit green and everyone felt their ears simultaneously pop.

"Helmets on," advised Dominic, jiggling his own into place. "Seal and pressurize."

All four pressed the same button on the front of their suits, and glass visors slid down over their faces. But as Becker reached for the reinforced door to the Master Bedroom, the excitement that was coursing through his veins was also tempered with apprehension. On the other side was the Glitch they'd been pursuing all night, and no one, not even Casey, seemed anxious to face it.

"Never be afraid to be afraid, boys," said Fixer Lake, double-pumping her Fists of Fury™. "Now let's go kick this little knocker's butt!"

Master Bedroom, Department of Sleep, The Seems

When they walked in the door, nothing was as they expected it to be. The foyer of the Master Bedroom was filled with a strange yellow glitter, almost like a fog, and Becker slowly let it roll through his orange-gloved fingers. There could be little question what it was.

"Sleep."

Though the Tireless Workers who manned this post were on duty 25/7[27], they were nowhere to be found. In fact, there was barely a peep, save the motorized hum of distant freezer units and the air conditioner above.

"I don't understand," whispered Dominic. "There's supposed to be a security detail here at all times."

By the front door were a series of hooks, each with a name label underneath it, but most of the Pajamas that usually hung there were already checked out. Simly stepped over to the employee time clock and pulled the most recent card.

"Roy Ponsen clocked in at 04:17."

That meant whatever had happened had happened just minutes ago.

"Are you feeling that?" asked Becker.

"Right where it hurts," answered Casey. Both of them were getting major pangs in their 7th Sense, but for the senior Fixer it was far more than that. Not only did the magnitude of the shiverings trouble her in a deep and serious way but also their familiarity.

"I hate to say this, but there's a lot of ground to cover and not a lot of time to cover it, so maybe we should split up?"

"Agreed," said Becker, studying the hallways that branched off from the foyer. The Master Bedroom was essentially a suite—a bunch of small satellite chambers (where the bathrooms and walk-in closet might be) surrounding central sleeping quarters—but instead of the requisite heart-shaped bed, in

27. The Seemsian day contains 25 hours (one extra, just in case).

185

the center stood the Seems-renowned Drowsenheim 4000. "I'll head for R & D."

"I'll check the output logs," announced Casey. "Simly, why don't you take Inventory?"

"Inventory? You mean, by myself?"

"No, I mean with the other Simly."

"What about me?" chimed in Dominic, in no hurry to go anywhere at all.

"You stay here by the door," ordered Becker, and this time the Administrator didn't talk back. "We'll let you know when we have something."

The trio gave each other the Shake for good measure, then headed down separate corridors and disappeared into the fog.

"Hello?" asked Becker, cautiously entering the area set aside for *Research & Development*. "Anybody here?"

R & D was where some of the brightest minds in the department tirelessly sought to perfect the formula for Sleep, and it was laid out like a think tank. There were couches to blow off steam, a ping-pong table, and a water cooler filled with Inspiration—all to foster brazen new ideas. And on a chalkboard was written a series of mathematical formulas:

$$S = (r + t)/S$$
$$I = ((Stress + Caffeine + Overthinking + \pi) * NSA)$$
$$Cure\ for\ I = S + (Pieces\ of\ Mind + Element\ J + ????)$$

From the look of the disheveled room, a session had recently taken place, but there was no one around, only a thin layer of yellow on the floor. On his belt, the Receiver began to vibrate on silent.

"Lake to Drane, come in."

"What do you got?"

"Nada."

"Me neither," but Becker saw several sets of footprints leading to the heart of the Master Bedroom, "at least not yet . . ."

BLIP . . . BLIP . . . BLIP . . . BLIP . . .

Over at Inventory Simly held his repaired Glitchometer and pointed it at the giant vats that stored the ingredients to Sleep. Refreshment, Twinkle, and Snooze were the three basic building blocks, and due to the ever-increasing demand for Sleep in The World, inventory had to be kept at the highest possible levels. But if the Glitch had infiltrated one of the drums, Simly's device was registering nothing.

BLIP . . . BLIP . . . BLIP . . . BLIP . . .

"Glitchometer my fat Seemsian tuchus!"

Simly angrily tossed the machine aside, resolving to never activate it again. Here he was, on a Mission with Cassiopeia Lake herself—whose poster adorned the wall of his dorm room at the IFR—and he had yet to do anything other than ask a bunch of stupid questions and spray a can of Raid.

"This is it, French Frye. If you can't come through now, you don't deserve to be a Fixer!"

Simly closed his eyes and once again tried to follow Becker's advice on how to activate the 7th Sense. He imagined he was the same schoolboy as before, except this time he was more specific, picturing growing up on a small farm in Dubuque, Iowa (for no apparent reason), where he rode with his father through the cornfields on a tractor, as in tune with the rhythms of Nature as humanly possible. He even went as far as visualizing himself crawling into bed, sunburned and worn out at the end of another long day, and ready for a much-needed Good Night's Sleep.

"Something's wrong in The Seems," he imagined desperately, like Becker or Casey or any other true Fixer might. "Now, isolate the feeling of where the Glitch could be."

But no matter how hard or how sincerely he tried, nothing would come his way. No feeling, no sense, no tingle, nothing.

"Frye to Fixer Drane," his hand despondently reached for his Receiver, "I got nothing either."

"Lake? Is that you, Lake?"

Back at the Decompression Chamber, Dominic's mind had begun to play tricks on him. As soon as the Fixers had disappeared, he'd become convinced that there was a small tear in his suit and had covered himself with masking tape and glue.

"Identify yourself!" He shouted at no one in particular.

The lack of response only served to further chip away at Dominic's fraying nerves. While his tenure as Administrator had been an uneventful one, there had also not been any major advances in the art. His greatest hope and the holy grail of Sleep had been to find the long-awaited cure for Insomnia, and he had driven his men hard, but the increasing sense of anxiety in The World (plus budget cuts) had conspired against any such innovation.

"I knew I should have stayed in Public Works! I could have had a nice fat desk job at the Flower Plant, but *noooo* . . . I had to be a big shot and transfer into Sleep!"

The worst part was, with annual reviews coming up and the Powers That Be looking to downsize at every turn, this entire fiasco could cause Dominic to be phased out entirely. He checked his beloved pocketwatch but that only exacerbated the problem, for Dawn was now only forty minutes away.

"Is that you, Lake? Is that you?"

Despite his bummedoutedness, Simly Frye kept his chin up and made his way over to Packaging. It was a low-lit room filled with long tables, measuring scales, and plastic bags exactly like the one revealed by the Glimmer of Hope. Each bag was filled with the same Sleep that coated the air, and hung on miniature hooks designed to carry them down to Central Shipping—but the assembly line had stopped dead. And so had the people who worked there.

There were rows and rows of them, all wearing protective Pajamas just like Simly's, but they were slumped over their posts and unmoving. The fog of Sleep was even thicker in here, and piles of the stuff had blanketed the ground and people like snow.

"Hello?" Simly could feel cold fear spreading through his belly. "Are you guys all right?"

They didn't look all right.

"What's wrong with you people?" The moment Simly touched one, the Tireless Worker collapsed to the floor and rolled onto his back. He looked dead to the world, his face hideously encrusted and air filter hopelessly clogged with thick yellow grime.

The Briefer backed away, beginning to hyperventilate, but he pulled himself together.

"Concentrate, Simly!" The Glitch had obviously been here on its path of devastation, but the question of where it was right now still remained. "You can do this."

For one final time, he closed his eyes and visualized his Iowan alter ego back in bed at the farmhouse of his youth. Listening carefully, he extended his awareness and picked up the sounds of the creaks in the floorboards, the swaying of the corn in the fields, and the groaning of the horses in the barn outside.

"Reach, Simly . . . reach . . ."

The moment was feeling real to him, realer than ever before. But it wasn't until he conjured up Rufus, the old family dog (who slept twenty-three hours of the day), walking into his bedroom with an unexpected spring in his step, that Simly felt something he had never felt before in his life.

A tiny chill on his arms that quickly traveled down to his toes. It was a feeling that almost spoke to him, whispering in his ear, pointing to the main Exhaustion Pipe that led to each of the individual packaging spouts. If that feeling was right, then the Glitch *was* still here. So he carefully removed a Safety Net™ from his Briefcase, and was about to pry open the pipe, when—**_WHOOSH!_**

A jet of yellow powder exploded from the pipe, shattering his glass visor and filling his lungs with Sleep.

"Help! Help me!"

But it was too late. His eyes were rolling back in his head and he was going into REM.

"Simly!" Casey appeared over his shoulder, catching him just before he fell. "Stay with me, Brief. Stay with me."

She reached into her Toolkit, pulling out a small balloon,

which Simly rapidly inhaled. Almost instantaneously he popped back up.

"What happened? Where was I?"

"You're okay, Simly. You just needed a Breath of Fresh Air™." Casey removed a helmet from one of the lifeless Tireless Workers and replaced it on Simly's head. "What happened?"

"The Glitch, Casey—it's in that Exhaustion Pipe!"

The Fixer hopped to her feet, but when she removed the epoxy seal, the only thing inside were cables and fiberglass tubes.

"If it was there, it's gone now." Her eyes followed the pipe, which snaked along the floor, up into the ceiling, and back to the center of the Master Bedroom. "But there's only one place left it can go."

The Drowsenheim 4000 was the latest in Sleep reactor technology and produced triple the quantity of its underwhelming predecessor, the Outkold 42. Still, the machine did the same dangerous job of synthesizing Refreshment, Twinkle, and Snooze into the precious salve known as Sleep. Its core was located behind eight-inch-thick glass, which protected those on the outside from any possible meltdown, but to Becker Drane it looked like a meltdown may have already occurred.

In fact, the Control Center before him looked like a scene out of a movie that he and Benjamin had watched one day on AMC called *The China Syndrome* (which had freaked his little brother out almost as bad as *Piñata*). Workers lay passed out everywhere—not just the reactor crew, but the Security Detail,

Packagers, and even some R & D types who must have come running when the alarms began to sound. Monitors and gauges were all in the red, and Sleep was burping out of the release nozzles in fits and starts, creating the ever-thickening yellow cloud in the air.

Worse yet, behind the glass the reactor itself was flickering and sparking as if ready to blow at any moment.

"Lake to Drane, come in, over!"

Becker picked up the Receiver. "Read you loud and clear."

"Get over to the Drowsenheim—I think the Glitch may be inside!"

"No maybe about it. I'm here right now and it doesn't look good."

"On our way."

Becker hung up his Receiver and turned to chapter 6 of his Manual. According to the sectional blueprints, the Drowsenheim was arrayed like a Russian Tea Doll, with one protective shell or "casing" inside another, inside another—all designed to protect the inner core from exposure.

"Let me have a gander." Casey arrived with Briefer Frye in tow and pointed to the center of the diagram. "There's still time to Fix it, but we have to stop the Glitch before it gets there—to the core."

"But the shells are rigged with magnetic trip wires!" cried Simly. "If anything touches the sides . . ."

"If it were easy, it wouldn't be fun." Casey winked at Sim, and he blushed like a schoolboy (from Dubuque).

"How do you want to handle this?" asked Becker, ready to follow Casey to the ends of The Seems.

"You tell me, #37. It's your Mission."

Becker grinned and picked up the gauntlet.

"Set up a Tool Table™, Simly."

"Aye, aye, sir."

Fixing has often been likened to operating on a human being, not just because of the self-evident stakes, but because of the slew of gadgets and Tools involved. Becker replaced his Pajama gloves with white latex as Simly spread out an array of silver instruments on the sterilized Tool Table top.

"Ready, sir?" The Briefer was fired up.

"Ready."

Simly cracked his knuckles, preparing to hold up his end of the bargain.

"Takerhöffer™!" demanded Becker.

"Takerhöffer!"

Simly handed Becker a pair of titanium forceps, which he used to undo the seals on the reactor's outer casing. Like she was handling fine china, Casey lifted off the first shell and placed it on the floor.

"Cutterhöffer™!"

"Cutterhöffer!"

With a small diamond-tipped scalpel, Becker cut four small holes in the second shell at equidistant intervals. Beside him, Simly suffered with every move.

"Lifterhöffer™!"

"Lifterhöffer!"

Becker inserted the four elastic prongs inside the holes and began to lift off the second shell. Immediately, a humming sound emanated from within—the sound of the casing's defense mechanisms. If he dropped it or the sides touched any other part of the reactor at all, that was all she wrote.

"You okay?" asked Simly.

The Fixer lifted higher, and the humming sound got louder, becoming a piercing whistle.

"Walk in the park."

Just as the noise threatened to split their eardrums, Becker finally pulled off the second shell, and everything went deathly silent. Underneath was a tangled forest of multicolored wires, snaking like vines over the final protective shell.

"I.C.U.™"

"I.C.U."

Simly handed Becker a monocle-like lens, and he placed it up against the reactor shell. A satisfied grin came across the Fixer's face, as the tool allowed him to see through the metal to what lay on the other side.

"There you are, you little son of a Glitch."

As if in response, a stream of Twinkle shot straight out at them, threatening to get in their eyes, until the liquid was quickly sucked up by the empty space in Casey's hand—her Portable Vacuum™.

"Carry on."

Becker nodded, then steeled his nerves for the final barrier.

"Those Things That Look a Lot Like Tweezers That You Cut Wires With™!"

Simly was about to repeat it, then just looked at Becker, like, "You gotta be kidding me," and handed them over. With remarkable quickness and precision, the young Fixer began snipping wires and working his way down to the core. But the closer he got, the more the reactor rattled and shook.

"It's going into meltdown!" cried Simly, frightened by the violence of the shaking.

"Not tonight it isn't."

Beneath the tangled mess was one final wire, tucked into a deep recess and seemingly impossible to reach.

"Dweezer Extension™."

But Simly was still frozen with terror.

"Dweezer Extension!"

Casey slapped Simly across the face.

"Thank you, sir. May I have another?"

"Just stay in the game, mate."

"Sorry, sir." Simly pulled the necessary Tool off the table.

Becker affixed the extension and lowered Those Things That Look a Lot Like Tweezers That You Cut Wires With deep into the recess, just like he had when he snooked the funny bone the last time he played *Operation*. Except this was no game.

"Now the second I snip this wire, get ready to move in." He blinked away the sweat from his eyes and prepared to make the cut.

But from within the Drowsenheim, a new sound emerged— something sparking—followed by a fierce blue light. It was now or never, so Becker squeezed the Dweezer's handle and split the final wire.

The last shell casing popped off . . .

There was a flash of blinding blue . . .

And finally . . .

Once and for all . . .

There it was . . .

The Glitch in Sleep.

Ripple Effect (Reprise)

"What were you expecting?" asked the Glitch, smugly flipping up its visor. "Some sort of two-bit Bleep?"

The Glitch was only four inches tall but with its scraggly hair, jagged-toothed maw, and mad, jaundiced eyes, it was certainly terrifying. The picture in Becker's Manual didn't do it justice, and it also didn't feature the curious aluminum jetpack strapped securely to its back. An acetylene torch extended from the pack and its owner was currently using it to carve a path into the reactor core.

"Freeze!" shouted Simly, holding it at bay with a Veiled Threat™.

"Anything you say, kid," sported the little monstrosity, dropping the torch and raising its hands in the air. The Briefer got ahead of himself, however, failing to realize (or remember) that Glitches are masters of deception—and have *three* arms, the last of which was surreptitiously reaching for a small button near its chest. "I don't want any trouble."

"Look out!" screamed Casey, as a thick cloud of black smoke belched from one of the tailpipes of its pack and filled the chamber. With Fixer Lake's Portable Vacuum already expended, she and the others had no recourse but to stumble through the smog and try to recover their bearings.

"Where is it?"

"Where did it go?"

The smoke was too thick to navigate, but they could hear something whirring like a helicopter all around them. And then—

"There!"

The Glitch had rematerialized *outside* the glass enclosure, a propeller extending from the top of its pack and over its tiny misshapen head.

"Fix this!"

It flashed the same vulgar gesture on all three of its hands, then zipped up into the rafters and disappeared from view.

"Drane to Night Patrol!" Becker pulled his Receiver off his belt. "Night Patrol, come in!"

"Night Patrol here, sir. We read you loud and clear!"

"The Glitch is on the loose inside the Master Bedroom. I repeat, nothing comes in or out of this room without a personal okay from me or Fixer Lake."

"Aye aye, sir!"

"And remember," Casey chimed in, "this bugger's got a few kangaroos loose in the top paddock, so don't try to wrestle it yourselves!"

"Understood!"

"Fixers over and out!"

Becker hung up while Casey pumped her Fists again, activating their ionic charge.

"C'mon, mates. This time we better stick together."

Glitches had been part of the system ever since back in the Day, and no one truly knew how or why they had originated—only that they were constantly gumming up the works. For countless years, they plagued Jayson and his ilk until the Powers That Be finally said enough is enough. Operation Clean Sweep (in which all Fixers and Briefers participated) was green-lit soon after, and by and large it was a rousing success—rounding up all but a few of the craftiest stragglers and locking them away in a maximum security prison.

What was the story behind this one, Becker wondered as the team fanned back toward R & D. Was it a new Glitch, never before seen, which heralded the coming of a second terrible onslaught? Or an old one, which had survived Clean Sweep and sworn revenge for that ignominious defeat? Regardless, it had to be neutralized, because a check of his Time Piece revealed that Dawn was less than thirty minutes away.

"We're running out of Time, boss!" whispered Simly. "If we don't get the Drowsenheim back online—"

"One step at a time," answered Becker, focusing on the now. "Glitch first, Drowsenheim second, then we save The World."

Casey hushed them both, then pointed straight up, as if she had a lock on their quarry. But unfortunately it was their quarry who had a lock on them.

"You're too late!" A voice dripping with insanity rained

down from above. "Sleep is mine! Then Nature! And soon I shall tear apart the very Fabric of Reality itself!"

Becker's mouth went dry as the Glitch's threat mirrored his own Worst Nightmare.

"The Plan is on my side this time, and there's nothing you can do to stop it! Nothing!"

Once again, a psychotic guffaw echoed from up above.

"Delusions of grandeur," said Casey. "This is gonna be just as easy as it was when we took down your mates during Clean Sweep!"

"Who dares to speak of that day? The agony of a thousand Glitches still rings inside my ears!"

"Don't worry, bitzer," needled Fixer Lake. "You'll be seein' them soon enough—when we take you back to Seemsberia!"

"Never!"

Incensed, the Glitch came rocketing down from the rafters.

The hunters scattered, and a chaotic battle of wills ensued.

The IFR's finest were at the top of their game, wielding the latest innovations from the Toolmaster—Sand Traps™, Spheres of Influence™, even Jayson's Invention™—but they had more than met their match in the Glitch.

Its Attak-Pak® was like an anti-Toolkit, stocked with every possible gadget and weapon imaginable.

"Simly, duck!" warned Becker, a second before the Briefer was ensnared in a Web of Deceit®.

"I'm okay," he mumbled through the fibrous strands. "Go on without me!"

The sight of his Briefer wrapped in gummy coils infuriated Becker to no end, and he whipped out his Return to Sender™ and hurled it at the Glitch with everything he had.

The fiend ducked, unaware that Becker wasn't actually trying to hit it, only to entrap it in the boomerang's magnetic pull. At first, the Fixer felt a surge of excitement as the Tool headed back with enemy in tow, but triumph turned to terror when the Glitch reversed the Attak-Pak's polarity and sent the projectile screaming back at its owner with twice the original speed. It caught Becker square in the chest and drove him violently backward, burying him deep in a mountain of Sleep.

"Who's next?"

Casey Lake's answer was to leap into the air with the help of her Jumping Jacks™ and catch the Glitch with a roundhouse kick to the face. When the imp recovered its bearings, the hatred of recognition was burning in its yellow eyes.

"You!"

Casey dropped to her feet and assumed a catlike stance.

"We meet again."

It was true. They had faced each other before—on the last day of Clean Sweep, when Casey was just a Briefer. That battle had nearly killed her, but when she regained consciousness between the Rock and the Hard Place, the Glitch had vanished, leaving behind only a single drop of blood.

"I've learned much since our last encounter, Lake."

"As have I."

They squared off like two mighty Ninja, preparing to settle an unsettleable score. And then, with a terrible fury, they attacked.

As the epic battle raged, sparks and shards of flying metal rained down upon Simly, who from his vantage point inside the Web of Deceit could only catch snapshots of the fray. Clouds of smoke and Sleep billowed all around him and it was impossible to see who was winning. He tried to find Becker in the melee but his Fixer was still lost beneath the pile of Sleep.

Suddenly there was a loud explosion, and everything went deathly silent.

"Casey?" called out Simly, searching through the rubble. "Casey?"

"I'm sorry, she can't come to the phone right now."

Only the Glitch remained, broiling with the lust of battle, and virtually unscathed.

"Can I tell her who's calling?"

Outside the Decompression Chamber, the Captain of the Night Patrol stood guard with his men.

"Stay focused, men. This is not a drill."

The security force known as the Night Patrol was made up of a small group of Sleep professionals, augmented by ordinary workers who volunteered mostly for the generous benefits package.

"I didn't sign up for this, Cap. I was only supposed to work two weekends a year."

"Well," said the crusty survivor of the Uphill Battle, "I guess you picked the wrong weekends."

BANG! BANG! BANG!

"What was that?"

The pounding on the door came from inside the Master Bedroom, prompting the Captain to immediately hush his squad.

"Identify yourself!"

"Open up, you idiot! It's me, Dominic, your boss!"

"Sorry, sir. We have strict orders not to let anyone in or out of that room without the personal sign-off of a Fixer."

"The Fixers have signed off—for good! Now open this door or you'll be dredging Sour in the Flavor Mines for the rest of your natural life!"

"Maybe you should open it, sir," suggested the rookie. "He sounds a little pis—"

"Shut up, son. For all we know, that could be the Glitch in there, impersonating the Administrator!"

The Captain considered his options, then shouted back through the door.

"I'm sorry, whoever you are . . ."

". . . but orders are orders!"

Back in the foyer, Dominic's heart sank.

"But you don't understand. They're gone . . . they're all . . ."

The sound of the whirring propeller returned to the Sleep-filled air and Dominic swiveled his head to see what was coming.

"Please! You've got to get me out of here! It's—"

"Leaving so soon?"

Materializing out of the haze came the miniscule abomination, and Dominic made a desperate run for it, but there was little he could do.

"Please! I just paid off my mortgage!"

As the Glitch dipped and dove, it pulled out a roll of duct tape and zipped around the Administrator, wrapping him from head to toe like a mummy. Dominic fell to the ground, unable to move or even speak, for the only part of his body uncovered were his eyes—open just enough to see the Glitch lowering a spinning circular saw blade directly toward his head.

"Time to take the dirt nap!"

Dominic's cries for help were muffled. No one could hear him scream, until . . .

"Hey, half-pint!" The Glitch turned to see a shrouded figure emerging from a cloud of yellow dust. "Why don't you pick on someone your own size?"

Fixer #37 stood his ground, bruised but undaunted, one hand poised behind his back and the other motioning for the Glitch to bring it on.

"With pleasure!"

Issuing a blood-curdling battle cry, the Glitch launched itself into the air and went hurtling toward Becker. It flipped a switch on its Pak, and dozens of weapons descended—swords, knives, scissors, even a Louisville Slugger borne by mechanical arms—but the Fixer refused to flinch.

The Greek philosopher Zeno of Elea is known primarily for his famous paradox, "What happens when an unstoppable force meets an immovable object?"[28] and the answer to this age-old riddle was about to be resolved. But at the last possible moment, Becker dove out of the way, narrowly escaping with his head still on his shoulders. As the Glitch whizzed past him, he rolled to his feet and finally pulled out the Tool he'd been concealing behind his back.

It looked like a spear gun, except instead of a point at the end, there was a large Kevlar hand, shaped like a baseball glove

---

28. À la K.I.T.T. vs. K.A.R.R.

or the hand from the Hamburger Helper box. Becker aimed and fired, and the hand exploded toward the Glitch, connected to the base via an extending metal cable.

The Glitch caught site of the projectile in its rearview mirror and tried to execute a dangerous barrelroll.

"Nooo!"

But it was a perfect shot.

The hand snatched the Glitch and roughly yanked it from its Attak-Pak. Then, with the touch of the button, the cord retracted like a tape measure, dragging the cause of all the night's troubles kicking and screaming back toward the Fixer, who nabbed it.

Ferdinand Becker Drane.

"Gotcha!"

Usually, when you're on a major odyssey to find something and you finally get it, it turns out to be a letdown because it's supposed to be "all about the journey" and stuff. But in this case, Becker had to admit he felt pretty gosh darn—

"Agghgh fhgjdu fh ejdgghd!"

The Glitch was trying to say something, but the index finger of the Tool was covering its mouth so Becker pulled it aside.

"Impressive," admired the Glitch. "I never saw this one in the Catalog."

"It's not in the Catalog," answered Becker. "I made it myself in Shop."

"What do you call it?"

"The Helping Hand.[29]"

"I hope you got an A."

---

29. Patent pending.

"C+."

"Bummer."

Even though they had just been locked in mortal combat, mutual respect seemed to pass between them.

"Well, kid, you got me."

Their conversation was cut short by the sound of the computer's voice echoing through the Master Bedroom.

"Alert! Alert! Arrival of Dawn in eighteen minutes. Alert!"

"Too bad it's not gonna do you any good."

Central Shipping, Department of Sleep, The Seems

The Foreman took another sip of his cold coffee and tried not to think about what might happen if the worst-case scenario came true. He snuck a private moment to open his wallet and look at his wife and kids on the day they all played hooky and went to Awesomeville, and it gave him strength for what he was about to do.

"All right, people, listen up!"

His entire staff was now on hand—all four shifts of the Seemsian day—and they were prepared to do whatever it took.

"Our people are up there right now trying to fix the Drowsenheim, but that's out of our control. All we can do is be ready when it goes back online—to get the Good Night's Sleep sealed, packed, and shipped to every person in The World!"

As a result of the Glitch everything had to be repackaged, because there was no way to tell which components in each box had been compromised in some way, shape, or form. The entire department had scrambled to get the new parcels ready, but they were still missing the one element that no Good Night's Sleep can do without.

"Everybody in position and wait for me to give the word!"

The Tireless Workers stepped to the rows of conveyor belts and assumed their posts. Before them were open boxes (labeled and addressed) and empty hooks that dangled in midair. Hooks that hopefully, Plan willing, would soon be carrying the priceless envelopes themselves.

"All set, #9?"

"Last time I double-fisted was the All-Nighter!" Over by the Main Hatch, Inspector #9 held up two fully inked stampers instead of one. "This is gonna be fun!"

"That's what I wanna hear."

Satisfied that his team was ready, the Foreman picked up his Receiver and called up to the Master Bedroom.

"We're all set down here, boss!"

Master Bedroom, Department of Sleep, The Seems

"Well done!" said Dominic, still trying to pull the last piece of duct tape from his mustache. "Stand by for further instructions."

Inside the reactor chamber, Becker was replacing the outer shell of the Drowsenheim and sealing the core up tight.

"Lightning Bolts™!"

"Lightning Bolts!"

Simly handed him four electric bolts, which instantly screwed themselves into place.

"All set," said Fixer Drane. "Let's blow this taco stand."

Behind the protective glass, Dominic was joined by Casey, who had taken the brunt of the Glitch's arsenal but lived to tell the tale.

"How you holdin' up, Lake?"

"Haven't had a beating that good since I tried to surf the Winds of Change." Casey chuckled appreciatively, then waited for Becker and Simly to get to safe ground. "Engaging Drowsenheim 4000!"

A deep rumble shuddered through the floorboards and the reactor coughed and hiccupped for a moment as if it might not turn over, but soon it settled into a peaceful hum.

"Well done, #37."

Casey gave Becker the thumbs-up, then grabbed the intercom.

"Lake to Packaging. The Drowsenheim is back online!"

"I repeat—the Drowsenheim is up!"

Over at Packaging, the Tireless Workers had finally awoken and stood poised to resume their duties.

"Affirmative! Packaging ready and waiting!"

Down the length of the ebonite table were rows of small faucets, and after a moment of gurgling, Sleep began to pump in perfectly apportioned amounts (Snooze levels lowered and Refreshment raised to account for lost Time). The Workers filled the sleeves once again, and the generator that sent the hooks toward Central Shipping kicked slowly into gear.

"Alert! Alert . . ."

". . . *Dawn arrival in 3.4 minutes. Alert!*"

"We're not gonna make it!" shouted Dominic, firing up the security monitor. "She's coming down the hall!"

On the small closed-circuit TV, a little girl with blond pigtails and a big smile was walking down a long corridor, escorted by Security Guards from the Big Building. In her hand was a slim attaché case, which contained the Plan for the brand-new Day. On her lapel, she wore a Badge, handwritten in red crayon, that simply stated: "Dawn."

"Stay frosty," offered Casey. "It's London to a brick that if the Good Night's Sleep gets out the door before she gets in, we're good to go."

Dawn could not slow down, of course, for once she left Sleep, she was then expected at Time and Weather and Nature and lastly at Miscellaneous, where the little bells and whistles were hung upon the branches of the Plan.

"Talk to me, Jonesy!" Dominic shouted into his Receiver.

Central Shipping, Department of Sleep, The Seems

"Central Shipping up and running!" reported the Foreman.

All around him, the Shipping floor was a bustle of activity—workers running to and fro, conveyor belts in motion.

"What about the Good Night's Sleep?"

Down at the Hatch, Inspector #9 was pumping like a steam engine, while long-anticipated packages were ejected into the In-Between and rushed over to The World.

"On its way, boss!"

"The Good Night's Sleep is on its way!"

Back at the Master Bedroom, the good news was greeted with sighs of relief, but they were not out of the woods yet.

"Did we get it out fast enough?" asked Simly, wondering if the Chains of Events had slipped beyond failsafe. "Did we stop the Ripple Effect?"

"We'll know soon enough."

Dominic pointed to the monitor where Dawn, under heavy guard, was in the process of exchanging Yesterday for Today. If the Good Night's Sleep had reached its destinations in time, then the Plans for the two days would match up, but if not . . .

"Warning! Chains of Events disassembling! Ripple Effect to commence in thirty seconds! Warning!"

"Hold on!" screamed Casey, as everyone grabbed on to the nearest something. Becker knew that in every department in The Seems the same exact scene was being repeated—terrified employees closing their eyes and whispering silent prayers—but in The World it was just the opposite. Sleeping or not, people were going about their business, completely oblivious to the fact that their lives could change irrevocably in a matter of . . .

"10 . . . 9 . . . 8 . . . 7 . . ."

"Anybody got any cool weekend plans?"

The others looked at Casey, as if *she* had a kangaroo loose in the top paddock, but she just cracked up like she was having the time of her life.

"6 . . . 5 . . . 4 . . . 3 . . ."

The computer stopped for a long, terrible, undisclosed amount of time.

Simly chewed his knuckles . . .

Dominic swallowed a Tums . . .

And Becker, for some reason, thought about the time his mom, dad, he, and Benjamin all went walking around Lake Mendota and found a four-leaf clover.

"Ripple Effect averted! Ripple Effect averted! Chains of Events reassembling! All systems proceeding as planned!"

Becker's heart started beating again, and he fell to one knee, overcome with relief. Casey grabbed Simly and planted a huge kiss on his lips (which nearly killed the poor Briefer and turned him a shade of crimson that Color Coordinators would kill to get their hands on). Amid the cheers and embraces, Dominic grabbed the departmentwide intercom.

"Attention, Department of Sleep . . ."

Central Shipping, Department of Sleep, The Seems

". . . This is your Administrator speaking!"

Down in Central Shipping, the staff stopped what they were doing, and even Inspector #9 had frozen in her tracks.

". . . the Ripple Effect has been averted!"

The room burst into joyful cries.

"I repeat . . ."

Night Watchmen's Station, Department of Sleep, The Seems

". . . the Ripple Effect has been averted and the Glitch in Sleep is Fixed!"

Among the revelry of his comrades, Night Watchman #1 took off his headset, sliding back into his Aeron chair, exhausted. Down on his Window, the Ice-Fisherman in Irktusk, the twins playing pattycake, even the Salesman in the small motel were finally fast asleep. And in Istanbul, Turkey, a young architect named Dilara Saffet had been jerked from her nap only minutes after it had begun. Strangely refreshed, she followed the scent of jasmine tea down the narrow stairs and out onto the street, not realizing that if she didn't turn around in a matter of seconds, she would literally collide with Atakar Bayat (aka Ati the Postman), who was scrambling to catch a mouse that had scared the donkey who dragged the cart belonging to the spice peddler's son.

The Night Watchman crossed his legs and put his hands behind his head and patiently waited for the final stroke to go down.

The Slumber Party, Department of Sleep, The Seems

Meanwhile, over on the east side of Sleep, the once-mellow Slumber Party had turned into a wild victory rave—strangers were hugging each other, weeping, promising that now that their prayers had been answered, they would definitely change their ways.

Back in the VIP area, however, a lone figure sat quietly in a private alcove booth. A host of emotions coursed through the ex-Candidate, prompting him to take another sip of his Certain Tea. On the one hand, there was everything he had sworn to do in the days that lay ahead, but on the other was the pride he felt for his old friend. The friend who would soon become his enemy.

"Way to go, Draniac," toasted Thibadeau Freck, raising his glass high. "Way to go."

A Dream Come True

Sleep Deprivation Tank, Department of Sleep, The Seems

Once the crisis was over, the Glitch was carefully transferred from the palm of Becker's Helping Hand to the Sleep Deprivation Tank, a secure holding cell in the basement of the department. It was now locked inside a carrying case, with holes in the side, providing proper ventilation and allowing the menace to speak, should it desire counsel or have any last requests.

"You like gadgets, right, kid?" At the moment, it was trying to reason with Simly, who had been instructed to keep guard over the creature while his superiors arranged for extradition. "The Attak-Pak? Take it! Just get me out of this box!"

"My orders are to hold you for shipment to Seemsberia."

"You don't understand," pleaded the Glitch. "This is all just a big misunderstanding. I'm on a Classified Mission from Quality Control to test the system and make sure everything's up to par. Here—the papers are in my back pocket."

The Glitch motioned for Simly to reach inside, but he was not so easily fooled and quoted from the Manual instead: "Page 103, Paragraph 2. 'Glitches are duplicitous creatures: crafty and persuasive. Never, ever listen to a Glitch.'"

"Especially this one," added Fixer Lake, as she and Becker stepped into the Tank with the Glitch's transfer papers in hand.

"Lake, you gotta believe me—it's not what you think!"

"Then what is it?"

"I tried to be good. I swear. After what happened between us, I said to myself, that's it, no more Glitching up the works. I gotta become a productive member of society."

Casey rolled her eyes as the Glitch's voice took on a conciliatory tone.

"I moved to the Outskirts, where I wouldn't be tempted to hurt anyone again. I even started a farm. We grew Fruits of Labor and zucchini and it was a good life—I mean, I was building something, right? Instead of destroying! But then . . ."

A dark shadow moved across its face.

"I started to get those . . . urges again."

Against his better judgment, Becker was actually starting to feel sorry for the Glitch, and Simly couldn't help it either.

"First, it was just a few innocent fantasies—a little mass destruction here or there—and I tried to bury myself in work. But no matter what I did, I couldn't get rid of the feeling that I was living a lie—that I wasn't being who I was meant to be! I mean, aren't I part of the Plan? And if everything in the Plan is good, then aren't I good, no matter what I do?"

"The Plan still allows for free will." Casey took a page

from the School of Thought. "Who and how to be is your choice."

"Then I choose to be . . . me!"

The Glitch started pounding on its cage with all three hands, gnashing its teeth, and spitting out expletives that cannot be reprinted herein. The assembled parties waited for the little ogre to finish its tantrum, but it never got the chance, for there was a knock at the office door.

"Don't worry. We'll take it from here."

Two Guidance Counselors from Seemsberia strolled in, exuding a pleasant and easygoing vibe. Unlike prisons in The World, Seemsberia is known for its success in rehabilitating wayward souls (though Glitches are some of the toughest Cases (yet also the most rewarding).

"Come now, Glitch. Is this really necessary?"

The Glitch finally took a breather from trying to trash its cell.

"I'll show you what's necessary, you two-bit quack."

The Counselors shook their heads, as if they had seen this kind of behavior before.

"Once we get you back in a more 'comfortable' setting, I think you'll find some of the new treatments most invigorating."

"Especially getting in touch with the Inner Child . . ."

"He works wonders."

Casey and Becker shook hands with the prison staff and the transfer of custody was complete.

"Fixer—don't let them do this to me," the Glitch was pleading with Becker. "They're gonna turn me into a marshmallow up there!"

"I'm sorry, bro, but it's for the best. You'll finally be able to get the help you need."

"But maybe I'm part of the natural order! How will you know if The Seems is working right if it's not constantly being tested by a Gli—"

But the door slammed, and with it, the Glitch's reign of terror had come to an unceremonious end.

"Well, I guess that's a wrap," chirped Simly. "Hoagies on me at the Briefer's Lounge."

"Not yet, Sim." Becker slung his Toolkit back over his shoulder. "There's still one more thing I have to do."

Dreamatorium, Department of Sleep, The Seems

Though the Bed Bugs and Pleasant Dreamers have always been kept in separate laboratories, the entire division of Dreaming had six months ago been put under the auspices of a new Vice President. At first, she was perceived as a corporate taskmaster, for Dreaming had always been a very casual operation where art was valued over science and dogs and foosball tables were *de rigueur*. But to the contrary, she turned out to be a very effective manager and showed the staff that productivity and creativity are not necessarily mutually exclusive.

"This is highly irregular," said the VP, intimidating in her gray pinstriped power suit. "Especially considering the charges that are pending against you."

"I know, ma'am," agreed Becker. "I'm hoping it might help my case."

"Call me Carol."

"This one is very close to my heart, Carol." Becker watched as she tapped her pencil on the table, debating the merits of his request. "I would consider it a personal favor."

That may have swung the balance, for such a thing from a Fixer is not so easily given.

"Okay," she relented, catching a strand of blond that had fallen out of her tightly pulled-back hair. "But there are some ground rules you'll have to follow."

"Understood."

"First, the so-called negative elements of a #532 cannot be removed from the sequencing. They're essential for creating the necessary emotional stakes, so the end-game of the Dream can have its desired payoff."

"Yes, that was my bad. I figured that part out after the fact."

Carol gave him a little extra stare to make sure the lesson had sunk in.

"Second, entering into a Dream World can be quite dangerous. It's a very seductive place, and you may find yourself experiencing the temptation to stay."

Becker promised to take that into account.

"Third and lastly, I'm sure you're aware of the restrictions of the Golden Rule, and given your obvious level of emotional attachment on this Case, I have significant concerns about—"

"I understand what you're getting at, Carol, but I assure you, it will not be a problem." Becker smiled, assuming his most professional demeanor yet. "I've already broken enough Rules for one night."

Carol seemed satisfied and checked the slim Time Piece on her wrist.

"Come with me."

Dreamatorium, Department of Sleep, The Seems

The Vice President returned Becker to the bubble room, where he'd made his critical mistake and where he hoped to have the opportunity to set the record straight. Towering above him was the Dreamweaver, again churning out the soapy amorphous realms that would soon be inhabited by the dreamers of The World.

"Give it a second, boss." Becker was accompanied by a junior Pleasant Dreamer, who had been assigned to help him construct a 532 to replace the one he had destroyed. "Back in High School still has a few more drops to go."

One of the canisters containing the golden dream fluid was still feeding into the machine and Becker patiently cradled his own container in his hand. Synthesizing the new 532 had been a surprisingly easy process, mostly because the basic solution was already premixed, but he had thrown in a few of his own special touches from the Spice Rack.

"You're good to go."

As a bubble floated by with a forty-five-year-old freshman trying out for the school play inside, the PD began to frisk Becker thoroughly.

"Watch the hands there, buddy."

"Just making sure you don't have any sharp edges."

The Fixer had stripped down to the bare minimum—not even his Badge—and with his track jacket and old school corduroys looked for all intents and purposes like a regular kid from Highland Park again.

"Anything else I need to know?" asked Becker.

"Just get out of there before she wakes up. Or else . . ."

"Got it."

The PD clicked Becker's canister into the machine, and the brightly colored fluid began to drain. It traveled down the filtration pipes, mixed with the soapy detergent, then slowly worked its way up to the billows, where it was finally expelled as a bubble with a fully realized world inside. Becker tucked his arms in tight and waited as the shimmering sphere gently floated toward his body.

"Here goes nothing."

Dream 532 (b)

Once he was fully engulfed, Becker opened his eyes and took in the reality that he, in part, had designed. It was the same playground that he'd witnessed before, with the same teachers chatting by the same wire fence and the same sounds of children permeating the air. Despite his training and experience, the Fixer had never been inside someone else's Dream before, and he was amazed at the attention to detail. The freshness of the air and the feeling of the sun on his face was as good, if not better, than the real thing.

"Who are you?"

Becker turned to see a fourth grader drawing a house in the dirt with a stick, who seemed shocked to have witnessed a kid with shaggy hair stepping directly out of a tree and into his lunchtime recess.

"I'm a Fixer from The Seems."

The child was dumbfounded (yet impressed), and Becker just winked and headed on his way.

To be honest, Becker had hoped to arrive *after* the bullying had begun so he didn't have to watch it happen all over again, but there was no such luck. It was even worse in person, as again the crowd gathered and the water balloon flew, and this time he could literally hear it slap her in the face. It took all of his combined Training to keep his composure and resist the urge to go down there and bust some heads, but he couldn't make the same mistake twice.

"See you later, alligator," said the meanest of the mean girls, and the mob begrudgingly dispersed.

This is where Becker had interceded last time and he watched as the girl with dirty blond hair and green eyes picked herself off the ground and found her way to a lonely bench. This time, however, someone came over to greet her.

"Is anyone sitting here?"

Jennifer Kaley looked up at Becker, her hair still wet and her eyes streaked from crying. She shook her head no, assuming this stranger was just another foe who'd come to add insult to injury.

"I saw what happened before."

"Yeah, so?"

"So, I'm sorry you had to go through that."

"Me too."

Jennifer didn't exactly seem interested in talking to some random kid, and after what had just taken place, Becker didn't blame her.

"Do you mind if I sit down?" the Fixer asked.

"It's a free country."

He took that as an invitation, then watched as the crow he'd inserted into the Dream as a nice distraction landed on top of the jungle gym right on cue.

"I'm Becker."

He reached out a hand, and after a long period of silent debate, she finally took it.

"Jennifer."

"Um . . . this is a little hard to explain, but you see . . ." There was no other way for Becker to say it. "I'm what they call a Fixer in this place called The Seems—which is this place that makes our World—and um, they were trying to send you a Dream tonight, but because of a Glitch in the Department of Sleep, they couldn't get it to you, and then by accident I popped your Dream because . . ."

Jennifer was looking at him like he was totally out of his mind, and Becker worried he was botching the whole thing.

"Sorry, I know it doesn't make a lot of sense . . . it's just . . . there was something special in that Dream and because of me, you couldn't get it. So they let me make a new one and deliver it myself."

Jennifer glanced around the schoolyard—the place that had been her own personal Nightmare ever since she'd moved from Vancouver to Caledon.

"You're telling me this is a Dream?"

"Yeah. I made it in The Seems."

"Then why did you make it so bad?"

"Well, it's about to get a whole lot better, if you want it to . . ."

Becker could tell that Jennifer wasn't quite buying his story, but she didn't exactly say no.

"Then follow me."

After a moment's hesitation, she finally got up from the bench, and Becker led her back in the direction of the trees through which he'd arrived. The kid in the dirt was still there, codesigning a two-car garage with a freckle-faced third-grader.

"Who's that?" asked the smaller of the two.

"No one. He's just a Fixer in The Seems."

The kids shrugged, as if that were all but obvious, then went back to their architectural plans. Neither seemed to notice that the trees that had once loomed over their shoulders were no longer there, having been replaced by a tall, wrought-iron gate—the kind that might adorn a deserted amusement park—complete with rusted turnstile that led to the other side.

"I've never seen this here before," observed Jennifer.

"I told you, this is a Dream," said Becker. "Anything can happen."

"Tickets! Tickets!"

A vintage ticket taker with a red, white, and blue carnival hat sat on a stool beside the turnstile, waiting for the only two customers of the day.

"Hey, Dr. Kole." It was Becker's English teacher, who he'd specially chosen for this part.

"Hello, Mr. Drane! I hope you have your tickets in hand, because I cannot allow our personal relationship to influence the performance of my duties!"

Becker pulled two shiny new tickets out of his back pocket and handed them over.

"Remember, the park closes promptly at dusk!" He ripped the tickets in half and handed one stub to each of them. "And be careful, my dear—this one's quite the ladies' man."

"Is that so?" Jennifer laughed, and for the first time since they'd met, Becker could feel her spirits lifting. He knew that was probably because she could glimpse what was on the other side of the gate.

"Shall we?"

Dream 532 was only ordered in the most dire of circumstances and it entailed the revealing of The Seems to a person in The World. It was only done inside a Dream because the aforementioned person was not actually being recruited for employment (in that case, they would have gone to Orientation), but rather needed a little help in negotiating the peaks and valleys of ordinary life. And even if they remembered everything that happened, they would no doubt write it off as a Dream, while hopefully the experience they had within would be memorable enough to change the way they looked at things when they woke up the next day.

The specific places that person visited in the dream varied on a Case by Case basis, but Becker wanted to give Jennifer "the deluxe." First, he took her to Time Square—the quaint town center in the Department of Time, complete with Second Hand Stores, Daylight Savings (FDIC), and Magic Hour—arguably the best coffee shop in the Seems. Then they stopped at the Sound Studio (where they design everything we hear) and the Olfactory (and all the things we smell) and they even dropped by the Weather Station, where Becker could show off a bit, because he knew the guys up there from a previous Mission.

"Briefer Drane," exclaimed Weatherman #3, upon seeing Becker with his wide-eyed companion.

"That's Fixer to you, Freddy!"

"Hey, congrats. How 'bout Yesterday? Was that a perfect day or what?"

"Keep up the good work."

Jennifer was impressed that Becker knew the people responsible for Weather, and she wasn't afraid to throw in a request of her own.

"Um, do you think you guys could do me a small favor?"

"For a friend of Fixer Drane . . . anything!"

"Well, I was just wondering if you could, like, bring down another ice age or something on this little town called Caledon."

"Caledon? Ontario, Canada? Sector 104?" The Weatherman quickly flipped through his log of local forecasts. "No Ice Age scheduled there for another thirty-two thousand years. How 'bout a Cold Spell? I could do that without having to get approval."

Jennifer laughed. "As long as I get a couple snow days out of it."

Becker knew where this was coming from. "Don't let a few bad apples spoil the bunch."

"Yeah. Sure. Right. I'm sure there's a lot of cool people I just haven't met yet." On the way out the door, though, she looked back and flashed Freddy the signal to hit 'em with everything they got, and the Weatherman gave her a thumbs-up.

But it was at the Big Building itself where Jennifer was really blown away.

Though it's strictly against the Rules to meet your Case Worker in person (even in a Dream), Becker made arrangements to stop by when the entire staff was out to lunch. While they rode the elevator up to the 423rd floor, Becker filled her in.

". . . and so each Case Worker has about twenty-five individual Clients that they manage, and their job is basically to help you in any way they can. Like sending you Happy Thoughts or nudging you down the right path, or in your Case, ordering up this Dream."

"And they let you design it?"

"The Pleasant Dreamers helped me out."

"That's a pretty cool job."

"Totally."

The elevator dinged and they wandered down the seemingly endless hallway to office #423006. A knock on the door confirmed that no one was there.

"C'mon . . ."

Inside the office was a messy desk with a nameplate: "Clara Manning, Senior Case Worker," and posted all over the walls were pictures of her Clients. You really have to love your people in this job, and it was clear that even though the two had never met, Clara felt that way about Jennifer.

One section of the wall was entirely devoted to her and there were Moments up there that Jennifer herself had nearly forgotten—like the time she had won a bronze medal at the Pacific Dolphin swim meet, and the time she hiked to the top of Hominy Hill and caught this amazing view of the valley and the church steeple and wished more than anything that someone could be there to share it with her. There was even a yellow Post-it note slapped on the corner of the laptop computer that read:

NOTE TO SELF: REMEMBER TO SEND J. K.
HINT THAT NECKLACE SHE LOST =
UNDER BED IN FLOORBOARD CRACK.

"This is wild . . . ," said Jennifer, staring at her life up on the wall.

"Yeah, Case Worker is a great job, but they have a lot of restrictions. They can't mess with your life or invade your privacy, but if you let them they can really help you out."

"Cool."

Clara had a cheap clock from Seems Club on her wall, and Becker noticed that another thing he'd preprogrammed into the Dream was about to unfold. He slid the window open and invited Jennifer to come to the edge.

"What are you doing?"

"It's a Dream—I figured we would fly to the next spot."

"Are you crazy?"

"Trust me." He reached out for her hand. "This is gonna be sweet."

She thought it over for a second, but everything else had gone pretty good so far, and someone told her once that when you fall in a Dream, you wake up before you hit the ground.

"Carpe diem," she said, and together they climbed out on the sandstone ledge. The wind was whipping back and forth, and far below they could barely make out the monorail, which looked like a toy train.

"What are we waiting for?" asked Jennifer, now fully on board.

"Hold on a sec." Becker had a giddy smile on his face. "I planned something special for 3 . . . 2 . . . 1 . . ."

Out of nowhere a song kicked in, as if playing on invisible speakers. Becker had debated between "I'm with You" and "Flight of the Bumblebee" when sifting through the music section of the Spice Rack, but had chosen "Sugar Mountain," because he expected a smooth and mellow flight.

"You like this song?"

"Totally."

"But isn't the guy who sings it, like, four hundred years old?"

Becker was bummed, because he'd thought it was a pretty good call.

"I could probably change it if you want?"

"No, I'm just teasing you." She smiled and punched him on the shoulder. "I love Neil Young."

They took one last look over the side before Jennifer leaped into the air.

"See you at the bottom!"

When they finally landed, they pretty much spent the rest of the day chilling out on the Field of Play and enjoying a first-class picnic. Twinkies were served with knife and fork, Soft Drinks™ provided as beverage, and outside of an Ultimate Frisbee game between the two sides of the Coin, they pretty much had the run of the place. Jennifer told Becker all about her gram and how cool she was and that even though it sucked that she had died, Jennifer always felt like she carried her around with her wherever she went. The whole time, Becker couldn't help thinking about how much she reminded him of Amy Lannin, which made him kind of sad but also made him kind of happy too.

Unfortunately, a Dream can only last so long, even though Time doesn't work the same way there as it does in Reality (you can spend six hours in a Dream and it's only two minutes of Sleep). And Becker remembered the Pleasant Dreamer's warning, so he knew it was almost time to wrap things up.

"Wow," said Jennifer, following the Fixer to the top of a craggy hill. "That's pretty awesome."

For his grand finale, Becker had chosen the Point of View, a thin jut of rock that overlooked the Stream of Consciousness. Soon, each would have to go back to their respective worlds, but neither were in any hurry to leave.

"I wish I could just stay here in this Dream forever," Jennifer mused, hair blowing across her face from the breeze.

"You can."

"What do you mean?"

Becker couldn't help noticing how pretty she looked to him—even more so than when he first "met" her on the Window in the Night Watchman's station—and it almost caused him to forget what he was trying to say.

"That's the thing about 532. It's supposed to make you feel better Tomorrow, not just Today."

"But tomorrow I have to go back to school." The harsh reality of Reality was creeping back into Jennifer's state of mind.

"But now it could be different . . . because now you know about The Seems."

"The Seems is just a Dream, Becker."

"No, it's not."

Jennifer gave him a look, like, "Dude, please give me a break."

"I swear!"

She could tell he wasn't kidding, and part of her wanted it to be true. In fact, a lot of her wanted it to be true, but there was still something bothering her about the whole idea.

"You know . . . if The Seems is so great and they have a Plan and everything . . . then . . . then why is this happening?" She was referring to her situation at school, which Becker had witnessed firsthand. "I mean, you don't know what it's like to wake up every day and know you're gonna have to deal with that."

Becker nodded and gazed down at the rippling water, as a single sculler whisked gently past them on the Stream. Somehow he knew this moment was coming. It came for him when Amy died and again when Thibadeau disappeared and sometimes it still came Today, when he saw all the things that didn't make sense in The World.

"That's a good question. And I actually asked my teacher at the IFR the exact same thing once, when I was going through a really tough time."

"And what did he say?"

"He said that no one, not even a Case Worker, can tell you what lies at the heart of the Plan—and beware of anyone who says that they can." Those were his Instructor's words verbatim, on the day when he was called off the Beaten Track to hear the tragic news about Thib. "But Fixer Blaque seemed to think it was something good."

Now it was Jennifer's turn to search for answers in the rippling water.

"I wish I could believe that."

"Well, that's the thing." Becker shrugged his shoulders. "Tomorrow, when you wake up, pretend that maybe The World

isn't what you thought it was. That the trees and the leaves and the wind—and even you—are all part of the most magical place ever created, and something, somewhere, is making sure you'll always be okay."

But Becker's new friend just rolled her eyes.

"Honest! I tried it and, yeah, it's not always easy, but the more you do it, the more you realize it just might be real." Becker kicked the dirt under the bench, trying to get the words out right. "Because sometimes you have to believe in something before it comes true."

Jennifer looked over at him with a wry grin, but she could tell he really meant what he was saying.

"Do you really think that'll work?"

"I know it will."

"But what if it doesn't?"

"Then I owe you another Dream."

There was so much more he wanted to tell her—like about the Plans for the Future and the Most Amazing Thing of All—but he didn't want to push his luck. He hoped that at least he had given her a little something that would make Tomorrow better than Today.

"Well, I'd better get going," said Becker.

"Is this the end?"

"Almost. But you'll remember everything that happened—or at least the important parts."

The sun had almost set now, cutting the Islands in the Stream across in shadow. They both got up from the bench and for the first time, Becker seemed a little awkward to Jennifer—not this mighty Fixer anymore, but just a boy, about the same age as her.

"Thank you for an amazing Dream." She leaned over and kissed him on the cheek. "Will I ever see you again?"

After spending the whole day with Jennifer, he realized how prescient the Dream VP's words were about the difficulties of adhering to the Golden Rule. But he couldn't tell her no.

"You can Plan on it."

She laughed and Becker slid his hands in his pockets, not sure what to do with either of them.

"Get going already!"

With a shy half-wave good-bye, the Fixer turned around and executed a perfect swan dive straight into the Stream of Consciousness. Jennifer cautiously leaned over the edge, hoping to catch a glimpse of Becker one last time . . .

But he never came up for air.

A Good Night's Sleep

The Stream of Consciousness, The Seems

Becker's head popped out of the water, gasping for oxygen, and he was still slightly disoriented from his entrance back into The Seems. The only way out of someone else's Dream is through the Stream of Consciousness, for it's the one thing that connects all of us to each other.

"Over here!"

By a small red boathouse at the edge of the water, Simly and the Pleasant Dreamer who'd helped Becker reconstruct the 532 were anxiously waiting for him to swim to shore.

"That was cutting it close, sir."

"You're telling me."

Becker stepped out of his wet clothes and they immediately

---

30. Superstition, a sub-department of the Department of Everything That Has No Department recommends against unauthorized use of the number 13.

wrapped him in a blanket, just to make sure he didn't catch a chill.

"So . . . how was it?" Simly wanted the juicy details, but the look on the Fixer's face said it all.

"Like a dream come true."

HONK. HONK.

Appearing over the bluff was Dominic Dozenski, at the wheel of a white golf cart, accompanied by Casey Lake.

"Good news, Drane!" He skidded the cart to a stop. "The Court of Public Opinion cleared you of all charges!"

In all that had happened, Becker had forgotten that his career was nearly in ruins. Dominic handed him a signed Writ, exonerating him of the Rule of Thumb Violation. And it was better still:

"By the power vested in me, I hereby commend Fixer F. Becker Drane for his work on the Glitch in Sleep, and present him with this Special Commendation." The Administrator handed Becker a glass orb, with a glittery substance inside. "An Ounce of Sleep!"

(That's a lot.)

"And to Briefer Simly Alomonus Frye"—Dominic pulled out a smaller-sized orb and delivered it to Simly—"half an ounce! Well done, son."

Stoked, Becker and Simly tucked away their prizes.

"Now I have to get back to Sleep, so if there's nothing else?"

"I think that's Mission accomplished." Casey hopped out of the cart. "And tell the Tireless Workers they were aces tonight."

"Will do. You all have a good night and I hope to never see

you again." Dominic quickly pulled a one-eighty and disappeared over a dune.

In the time since they'd repaired the broken Drowsenheim, Casey had a chance to shower and change into something more comfortable. Now she was wearing a sundress and sandals and looked ready for a bonfire or a dinner at a beachfront café.

"Nice work, #37," Casey congratulated him. "And you too, #356. How 'bout I spring for burgers over at the Flip Side?"

That sounded great to both of the tired repairmen. The Flip Side was a beachfront burger joint owned and operated by retired Fixer Flip Orenz, who had hung up his Wrench for a spatula. It had tasty views and a tastier menu and had instantly become the hangout of choice for Fixers and Briefers alike. But Becker had a conflict of interest.

"I wish I could go with you guys, but I've got this quiz tomorrow and I haven't studied at all."

"Why don't you let your Me-2 take the quiz?" suggested Simly. "I'm sure it could get you at least a B."

"I would love to, trust me—but I couldn't do that to my English teacher."

The Briefer dropped his head, feeling the taste of the savory cheese fries slipping away.

"Are you sure we can't get you to reconsider?" Casey pushed a little harder. "There's supposed to be a good crowd tonight."

"I hate to say it, Case—but I gotta take a Rain Check."

Fixer Lake was bummed but respected Becker's dilemma. "I guess it's just you and me, Simly."

"Sorry, sir, but protocol says the Mission isn't over till the Fixer hits the Landing Pad."

It killed Simly to say it, but the fact that he and Casey Lake were now on a first-name basis more than made up for the pain. (Wait 'til the guys on Third Reeves heard about this!)

"Suit yourself. But I'm gonna go grab myself an In-Between Burger—'animal style!'" Casey took her freshly cleaned hair and tied it in a knot, then headed for the water taxi that passed directly by Flip's. "Live to Fix, mates!"

"Fix to Live!" they replied.

And with that, Casey Lake was gone.

"She really is the best, isn't she, sir?"

"Yeah." Becker proudly put his arm around his Briefer's shoulder. "She really is."

Customs, Department of Transportation, The Seems

The lines in the Terminal had finally died down and it felt like a lifetime ago since Becker was there. Both he and Simly needed to come down from the Mission, and since they had a few extra minutes before Becker's Departure, they stopped at the Food Court to grab a little chow.

"Great job, kid!" shouted the guy behind the counter of Out-of-This-World Wok. The teenage girl making pastries at Seemsabon was also duly impressed, and she wrote her phone number in frosting on one of the cakes.

"Call me sometime."

Simly assumed that she was talking to Becker, but the Fixer insisted he had it all wrong.

"No, dude, she was totally digging you!"

"Really?"

"Heck, yes. If you don't call her, I will."

Simly horked the digits out of Becker's hands and swore to himself that this time he would finally get up the courage to dial.

"So, there's one thing I still can't figure out," Becker admitted, carrying his tray to a two-top.

"What's that, sir?"

"Back in the Master Bedroom . . . how did you get a read on where the Glitch was hiding?"

The Briefer shrugged, as if there were only one explanation.

"L.U.C.K."

"The residue of Design." Becker laughed, and Simly couldn't argue with that.

"Seriously, sir—thank you for your advice about the 7th Sense. It might have been my imagination, but I could have sworn I felt something back there."

"I'm not surprised, Sim. You've got the skillz to pay the billz."

That meant everything to Simly.

"You too, sir. You did an awesome job."

"Muchas gracias."

Up on the Departures screen, Becker Drane's name was moving toward the front, and soon he would be cleared for entrance back into the In-Between.

"I guess this is it, dude." They got up from the table and dumped their trays in the receptacle marked "Trash," which would soon be recycled into Good Energy. "Now don't forget to take care of that one last thing we talked about."

"No problem, sir. Simly Frye is on the job."

"Passenger F. Becker Drane to Landing Pad for Seems-World Transport. Passenger F. Becker Drane."

Simly snapped to an official Salute.

"Briefer 356 signing off!"

"It's been a pleasure serving with you, Frye!"

"The pleasure was all mine."

The final boarding call sounded again and so the two parted ways, Simly back toward his dorm room on Third Reeves and Becker to the Landing Pad, to make the return Leap. The end of a Mission is always bittersweet, because on the one hand you're psyched to bask in the glow of a job well done, but on the other, you know it might be a while before you get called in again. Becker wished that he could drag it out just a little bit longer, at least long enough to see the look on his old Instructor's face, but Worldly concerns were calling, so he cued up his Mission Mix to track #9, snapped on his Transport Goggles, and pulled the straps up tight.

Office of the Head Instructor, IFR, The Seems

The sound of keys jangled outside the thick cherrywood door, and in walked the imposing figure of Fixer Jelani Blaque. His IFR mug spilled steam off the top, and he was still on his Receiver with his wife.

"I'm not sure what time I'll be home, honey. We're going through the new SATs this evening and we might have to burn some Midnight Oil."

Fixer Blaque had relocated from The World to The Seems after his retirement from active duty, and now lived with his family in the coveted Head Instructor's Cottage on the grounds of the IFR.

"Do you want me to send you a care package from Mickey's?" asked Sarah Blaque, referring to her husband's favorite deli.

"Only if they have the good pastrami."

"I'll see what I can do . . ."

"You're my hero. (No pun intended.)"

Blaque hung up, thankful beyond thankful that he had walked into the Department of Health that day and met the pediatrician who became his betrothed. He had spent many months in the hospital following "Hope Springs Eternal," for the completion of that Mission did not come without a price. But few of his colleagues (and none of his Candidates) knew the secret that lay behind the blue-tinted Eye Glasses™, which had been specially designed for him by Al Penske himself.

The retired Fixer sat down, dwarfed by the massive stacks of paper that Human Resources had piled on his desk. He was about to pull the first one off the top when he noticed something else amid the clutter. Blaque reached out and picked up the small glass orb with his callused hand, along with the note that was left underneath it.

Dear Fixer Blaque,

I just completed my first Mission, and thanks to you, it turned out okay. It wasn't just the Glimmer of Hope you gave me (though that came in pretty handy too) but everything you ever taught me. I felt like you were there on the Mission with me, every step of the way, which is why I wanted you to have this. I know those Candidates can sometimes cause a lot of sleepless nights...

Take care and give my best to Sarah and the kids.

F. Becker Drane (aka #37)

Blaque shook the little container and listened to the sound of the dust sifting back and forth inside. Becker was not the first Fixer he had trained, nor would he be the last, but that didn't make it any less satisfying. He allowed himself to savor the feeling for just a brief second before his own Training took hold, as it always did. He focused back into the Now and pulled the first Seemsian Aptitude Test off the highest pile.

Name: Shan Mei Lin
Address: No. 23 Shifuyan Dongcheng-Qu, Beijing, China
Telephone (optional): (Lin never gave out her cell)

Fixer Blaque put his feet up on his desk, then quietly began to read.

Outside the Instructor's office, Briefer #356 smiled with his own satisfaction and headed back up to his dorm room. Now that he had delivered Becker's message, he needed to catch some shuteye of his own, but there was still one more thing *he* wanted to do.

Simly picked up the phone and punched in Crestview 1-2-2.

"Grandpa?"

It took a second for Grandpa Milton to put in his Hearing Aide™, because he was getting up there in years.

"Simly? Is that you?"

"Yeah, Grandpa—it's me. I just got back from my Mission." Simly closed his eyes and allowed himself to relive that moment in the Master Bedroom, when a set of chills had shot from his arms down to his toes. "You'll never guess what happened . . ."

30 Custer Drive, Caledon, Ontario

Cool Canadian air blanketed the town of Caledon, and all of the intrepid night owls who walked the streets and filled the pubs and restaurants had packed it in for the night. But in the bedroom on 30 Custer, Jennifer Kaley had only been asleep for thirty minutes when she awoke with a start.

"Whoa."

It was one of those dreams that you remember with utter clarity and are almost caught inside of when you first wake up. She could still hear the gulls in the sky and feel the breeze off the Stream, and she tried to put her head back down on the pillow and get back into it before the real world rushed back in. But it was too late, because she felt more wide awake than ever.

Jennifer rolled over and looked at the clock, which read 4:32 a.m., and she couldn't believe that everything that happened inside her dream had taken place in a half hour (for it had seemed like a jam-packed day). Part of her thought about the boy in her dream and how odd it was that she had dreamed about someone she had never met before (though he was kind of cute). And the other part thought about everything he'd shown her and everything he'd said about this world and how it was connected to that one.

"What was the name of that place again?" she asked herself, but she couldn't for the life of her remember.

Almost immediately, Jennifer started to get depressed, because it was all beginning to fade—not just the scenery, but everything they had talked about and done. Only four hours from now there would be that awful moment of getting off the bus and walking into Gary Middle School, wondering who was going to pick on her this time. The kid in her dream had tried to tell her something that was supposed to make her feel better, but she couldn't remember that either, and whatever good feelings she had after she woke up slowly melted away.

She buried herself under her down comforter as if to hide, but even the soft goose feathers could not protect her from the day to come. Jennifer had almost completely forgotten everything that had happened to her inside her 532 when—

"Waittaminit!"

She dove off the bed and ran to her closet to look for a flashlight, which she found amid her camping gear. As she hit the black button, Jennifer hoped like anything that the batteries still had some life in them, and when a weak beam trickled out, she pointed it under her box spring.

"Be there . . . be there . . ."

The only memory she had left of the dream was of the Post-it note, stuck on the laptop computer in her Case Worker's office. But it couldn't have been real . . .

"If you're there I promise to eat Brussels sprouts for two—"

The moment her fingers slid into the small crack in the

hardwood floor that she had no idea was there, she knew. Even *before* those same fingers closed upon the silver necklace with the locket on the end.

Goose bumps running down her arms, she stood up and went to the window and looked out with wonder at the streets of Caledon. As she started to remember some of the places she had "visited" that night and some of the things that boy had told her, The World *did* look slightly different. And if the Post-it note were real, then maybe, just maybe, her dream was real. And if that was real, then . . .

Jennifer Kaley put the last present her grandmother ever gave her back around her neck and got into bed.

"The Seems! That's what it was called." She smiled and closed her eyes. "The Seems."

12 Grant Avenue, Highland Park, New Jersey

All was quiet and dark in the bedroom of the older of the two Drane children, save for the sound of intermittent snoring. Becker #2 rolled over in his bed, blissfully asleep—and completely unaware that Becker #1 was on his way back up the elm tree outside his window.

The Fixer climbed in, trying not to disturb his sleeping counterpart, but the Me-2's auditory alarms were immediately tripped.

"Hey, dude," it said, popping up in bed. "How'd it go tonight?"

"Not bad for my first Mission." Becker shut the window behind him and dropped his Toolkit on the floor. "You?"

"A little fun and games with Benjamin, but nothing I couldn't handle."

"Well, I'm sorry to deflate you," Becker apologized, "but I need to get a Good Night's Sleep myself." That wasn't going to be easy, considering it was already 4:45 a.m., and he hadn't even begun to study for his quiz.

"No problem. It was nice being you, if only for a little while."

"Cool. I'm sure you'll get another chance soon."

Becker flipped the dial on the back of its neck to "Off" and air began to hiss out of the release valve.

"Oh, by the way—I almost forgot." The Me-2 was already half the size of its previous self. "I left you a little something by the . . ." but it crumpled before it could finish the thought.

Becker gently rolled the Me-2 into a ball and stuffed it back into his Toolkit, then listened throughout the house, just to make sure that his work on the other side had had its desired effect over here. His mom and dad were certainly conked out, but there was still a light on in Benjamin's room. When Becker opened the door, he found his little brother passed out among his easels and brushes, a crayon in his hand. He was almost finished with the picture the Me-2 had assigned—a drawing of a Fixer saving the day—and Becker couldn't help but get a little choked up when he saw the heroic portrait of #37.

"Yo, Beavis—get back in your bed!"

But the child was completely out cold.

The same could be said for the rest of Highland Park, for when he looked out the same second-story window that earlier had revealed so much trouble, the neighborhood was quiet and the lights dimmed to black. Even Paul the Wanderer was happily sawing Z's in the backseat of his Cutlass Sierra, a dog-eared copy of *Infinite Jest* resting on his chest.

"Sweet."

Everyone else in The World had been taken care of, and so now it was time for Becker to get a little R & R himself. The only problem was, he was totally unprepared for the day to come, which was starting to become a regular occurrence. He remembered his mother's admonition about only being able to save The World if it didn't get in the way of his studies, but he was so tired that the thought of reading even one of the "Best Books Ever" was more than he could stomach. There was a slim chance that he could cram during homeroom, but he was already contemplating his latest alibi when he noticed something sitting on his desk.

Tucked inside the brand-new copy of Dr. Kole's weekly selection was a single slip of paper, covered with handwriting that was eerily similar to his own. It read:

Likely questions and answers for quiz on I Am the Cheese.

"Nice job, Me!" Becker made a mental note to activate the Me-2 the next time the family did something fun, like go to Carolier Lanes or even Point Pleasant. He set his alarm clock for 7:30 sharp, slapped on his pajamas (not the kind that protect you from hazmats), and finally, *finally*, got into his own bed.

"Ahh . . ."

There was nothing like the feeling of getting under the covers after a long night's work, especially when you know firsthand all the goodies that are coming your way. A fresh-baked Yawn slipped out of his mouth, and he pulled up his blanket and dug his head into the pillows. What a Mission it had been—a Glitch on his first time in the big leagues. Who would have thought?

It was impossible for Becker not to replay all of the evening's adventures in his mind, from the moment his Blinker went off to seeing Thibadeau again to making someone else's Dream come true. But thankfully, the Zonker 111 he'd installed at WDOZ was doing its job, for he could feel the waves of Slumber calling him back home.

This time, there would be no tossing and turning—no repositioning the legs, no turning the pillow over to make sure the other side was cool. Only that soft, sweet paradise just before . . . before . . .

Central Shipping, Department of Sleep, The Seems

The rhythmic sounds of the conveyor belts had replaced the whooping alarms and chugged in perfect time with the sounds of Inspector #9's stamp. Though she wasn't double-fisting anymore, that didn't mean she took her job any less seriously.

"Hold on a second!" The row of boxes clipped to a halt as she picked one off the line and flattened out the address label so it wouldn't peel away during transit. "All right, fire it up!"

Two behind that one was another package filled with its own unique contents, just like all the rest. Inside were the combined efforts of the Tireless Workers, the Pleasant Dreamers, and the Snorchestra—all in close coordination with Case Worker #15443, who had never met the person to whom this box was addressed but cared about him deeply just the same.

F. Becker Drane
Sector 33-514
12 Grant Ave.
BEDROOM #2

With a heavy hand, Inspector #9 stamped the package for shipment, and the final barrier to exit had been crossed. The Hatch light turned green, the door to the In-Between slid open, and at long last, Becker's Good Night's Sleep was on its way.

The Hatch door noiselessly closed and the next package came up for delivery.

Epilogue

The Flip Side, Safe Harbor, The Seems

Casey Lake tipped the water taxi driver and stepped onto the rickety dock that led to the Flip Side. Draped with Christmas lights and featuring live calypso three nights a week, the beachfront burger joint was reserved for a private party on this occasion, as evidenced by the sign that had been tacked to the thatched roof of the hut:

CONGRATULATIONS, BECKER!

A smattering of patrons were gathered, for though the message had been Blinked regarding the postponement of the traditional first-Mission surprise party (to a nonschool night), a few Fixers and Briefers (and one Agent of L.U.C.K.) were willing to celebrate with or without the young man of the hour.

"Nice job, Lake," said No-Hands Phil from his stool at the counter. "I skipped a pig roast on Jost Van Dyke to come to this!"

"I tried," replied Casey, ordering her burger medium rare. "The kid's serious about his schoolwork."

"Don't mind Phil." At a table overlooking the water, the Octogenarian was locked in a serious game of mah-jongg with her friend Tony the Plumber. "He's just jealous that Drane got a Glitch and he got a Cloud of Suspicion."

"Jealous, my butt. I coulda Fixed that Glitch with my hands tied behind my back."

"I didn't think you had any hands," cracked Tony, resting his cards on his generous belly.

"Ha, ha," grumbled Phil, then continued griping to Flip by the grill. Contrary to popular belief, Phil actually had hands, but he claimed to Fix so well he didn't need them (as in "Look, Ma! No hands!").

Down by the water, the mighty Li Po cast another reel and waited for the telltale tug of a Compliment or Fluke. Though his face was tranquil and serene, he knew of the ominous day that was approaching. But since he had not spoken a word in more than twenty-five years, he allowed the one to whom he'd passed the Torch to speak instead.

"So have you guys heard the news?" asked Casey, taking a seat at the table with Fixers #3, #26, and #31. "And I don't mean Becker not making the party."

"What news?" asked Tony, not looking up from the tiles. "We didn't get any Blinks."

The Octogenarian shook her head.

"I only heard because I bumped into someone in The Know on my way here." Casey pulled her chair in closer, and her face unexpectedly darkened. "Apparently, while we were all caught up in this Glitch thing, someone made off with fifty trays of Frozen Moments from Daylight Savings."

"Someone?" But the Octogenarian knew exactly whom she meant. "What would they want with those?"

"By themselves, nothing. But combined with enough fertilizer, and if they're ever able to get their hands on a Split Second . . ." Casey's voice dropped to a whisper. "They might have the necessary components to build themselves a Time Bomb."

Suddenly, no one was hungry anymore.

"Mama mia." Tony slouched in his chair and threw his hand on the table. "And I was just about to drop the kong."

"Tell me about it." Casey's eyes gazed out over the cove. She wondered how things had gotten so daggy in The Seems, and what they were going to do about—

"Look on the bright side, everybody." The Octogenarian, no matter what problem she faced, always maintained her sunny disposition. After all, she had made it back from the Point of No Return and claimed victory at the Jaws of Defeat. "The rise of The Tide just means our Missions are going to be that much more fun."

Her tablemates glanced at each other, wondering if the old lady had finally lost her marbles—but then they realized she was right. Fixers weren't in this business because it was easy. They were in it because it was hard. And the harder the better.

"To the Time Bomb!" Tony the Plumber raised his vanilla shake. "And to whoever's lucky enough to Fix it."

The others hadn't ordered drinks, so they clinked their burgers instead. Even though no one would ever hope for such a thing to happen, all three secretly wished that if it did, they would be the one to get the Call—for on such Missions are legends made.

"To the Time Bomb!"

Glossary of Terms

7th Sense: An innate sense or feeling that something in The Seems has gone wrong and will soon affect The World. Fixers often use this skill to track the location and/or nature of a Malfunction.

Agents of L.U.C.K: Members of a covert team charged with spreading the life-changing substance to its appropriate Sectors in The World. (*See also* L.U.C.K.)

Alphabet City: The urban center where much of the Seemsian workforce live. Once an edgy neighborhood, property values have skyrocketed as a result of gentrification.

Awesomeville: The most popular amusement park in The Seems. Attractions include: an Awesome Place to Eat, Awesome Things to Do, and the Most Awesome Ride Ever.

Beaten Track: A once popular hiking trail weaving throughout the entire Seems. Due to a series of unfortunate incidents, it is no longer considered safe after dark.

Beyond: A tract of soupy marshland, newly redeveloped and soon to be available for waterfront/condominium living.

Big Building: The colossal structure in the center of The Seems that houses all of upper management, including Case Workers and the Powers That Be.

Black Market: A weekend fleamarket held on the Outskirts of The Seems and featuring Goods and Services nearly impossible to attain via ordinary means. *Caveat emptor!*

Bleep: A small, pesky creature indigenous to The Seems that is wont to nest within Departmental machines.

Blinker: The multifunction communication device carried by Fixers and/or Briefers.

Blip: A power surge or spike, often causing an interruption in departmental services. Blips are a very serious Malfunction indeed, often reflecting larger structural concerns.

Blunder: A Malfunction attributed to employee error.

Briefcase: A Briefer's Toolkit, albeit with less Tools and Space.

Briefer: The right-hand man or woman to a Fixer.

Candidate: The name given to a student at the IFR; one engaged in the process of becoming a Briefer, and perhaps someday, a Fixer.

Case(s): The confidential file(s) kept on each person in The World.

Case Worker: A high-level official charged with monitoring and/or encouraging the progress of persons in The World.

Catalog: The four-color publication (often found in bathrooms at the IFR) showcasing the latest in Tools, gear, and miscellany available for Fixer and Briefer use.

Central Command: The 24/7 HQ of Fixer operations.

Chain of Events: An interconnected series of links, or "things that happen," strung together under meticulous conditions and composing the essential building blocks of the Plan.

Clearance: One's level of access in The Seems.

Coin: Consisting of the Heads and the Tails, two rival philosophical gangs (aka Cost/Revs) continually fighting over the most vexing issues of the day.

Color Wars: A dark era in Seemsian times when the color palette for The World was being decided. Fierce battles erupted, pitting brother against brother, Green and Blue against Purple and Red, and though a truce was ultimately reached, three of the most beautiful colors ever mixed were lost forever.

Compendium of Malfunction & Repair, The: The technical volume containing "everything you need to know to Fix." Also known as: "the Manual."

Court of Public Opinion: The feared governing body of The Seems charged with drafting and enforcing the Rules.

Day, the: The time before the beginning of Time when The World was under construction.

Degree of Difficulty: The number system ranging from 1 (easiest) to 12 (hardest) to denote the level of complexity of a Mission.

Department: A specialized area in The Seems responsible for a particular element of The World.

Door: A portal or access point leading from The World to The Seems.

Fabric of Reality: The thin, virtually invisible filament that surrounds and protects The World.

Fixer: A highly trained specialist called upon to repair Malfunctions that might put The World at risk.

Flip Side: 1. Slang for whichever side (The World or The

Seems) you are not on. 2. A beachfront burger joint owned by ex-Fixer Flip Orenz that is frequented by Fixers and Briefers alike.

Frozen Moments: Pristine moments of Reality preserved at below-zero temperatures in the Department of Time.

Future Oriented: A brain trust of some of the foremost thinkers in The Seems, tasked with charting the best possible course forward.

Glitch: A small but lethal nuisance that can wreak havoc in The Seems and hence cause mass destruction in The World.

Golden Rule: "No employee, agent, or advocate of The Seems having accessed (or with access to) the confidential Case File of a person in The World may engage in contact, communication, and/or relationship with said person, romantic or otherwise."

Here, There, and Everywhere: Three of the more popular suburban neighborhoods in The Seems (aka "the Three Towns").

Highland Park: 1. Becker Drane's hometown. 2. "A Nice Place to Live."

Holding Tank: A maximum-security prison housed in the frozen wasteland of Seemsberia. Incarcerated luminaries include: the Insomniac, Justin and Nick F. Time (aka the Time Bandits), and the Chain Gang.

Human Resources: The division in The Seems responsible for recruiting persons from The World for those jobs that require it.

In-Between: The space separating The World and The Seems through which all Goods and Services flow.

Institute for Fixing & Repair (IFR): The state-of-the-art facility in The Seems responsible for training all Briefers and Fixers.

Jaws of Defeat: Somewhere you don't want to go.

The Know: A shadowy Seemsian clique trading in illicit information—often pilfered from the Big Building or Future Oriented.

Leap: The tumultuous journey from The World to The Seems, or vice versa.

Lost and Found: Where things go when you can't find them.

L.U.C.K. (little unplanned changes of kismet): A thin residue generated during the process of designing Reality. Contrary to popular belief, the substance is always good. (*See also* Agents of L.U.C.K.)

Manual: *See The Compendium of Malfunction & Repair.*

Mechanics: Employees/staff at the IFR.

Middle of Nowhere: The only location in The Seems that is off-limits to everyone, regardless of Clearance.

Mission: A job or assignment embarked upon by a Fixer or Briefer, usually accompanied by great stakes.

Mission Inside the Mission: An IFR term referring to the smaller, more personal stakes to which a Fixer must often cling in order to complete the challenges of a Mission.

Most Amazing Thing of All: The most amazing thing of all.

Naming Convention: The invite-only gathering toward the End of the Day, at which the names for The Seems and The World were decided.

Outskirts: A far-out area of The Seems that vagabonds, bohemians, and dropouts from mainstream Seemsian society call home.

Personality Scan: A highly advanced method of identity verification, thought to be 100 percent accurate.

Plan, the: The organizing principle upon which The World is run.

Point of No Return: Somewhere else you don't want to go.

Powers That Be: The council of the twelve highest-ranking officials in The Seems.

Practical: The grueling, wheat-and-chaff separating, hands-on, feared and revered comprehensive examination that all Candidates must endure (and pass) before being allowed to Brief (or Fix) in the field.

Quality Control: The division in The Seems responsible for making sure that The World is being built with the highest-quality standards in mind. Random inspections may often be conducted with regard to color, crispness, variety, etc.

Radar: The towering convex satellite dish through which information is broadcast to The World. Drifters and seekers are known to hang out under it, hoping to catch wind of something cool.

Ripple Effect: A large-scale unraveling of the Plan, often caused by broken Chains of Events.

Rotation (aka Duty Roster): The list of Fixers currently on active duty.

Rulebook: The text containing the sometimes burdensome set of regulations that govern behavior in The Seems, including the Golden Rule, the Rule of Thumb, the Rule That Was Made to Be Broken, et al.

School of Hard Knocks: Chief rival of the School of Thought, this institution caters to the more practical-minded students and those anxious to enter the workforce.

School of Thought: Chief rival of the School of Hard Knocks, this institution caters to the more ethereal-minded students and those not anxious to enter the workforce.

Scratch: The basic building block of all things.

Sector: A geographically outlined section of The World.

The Seems: The place on the other side of The World responsible for generating what you see outside your window right now.

Seemsberia: A vast expanse of frozen tundra on the far reaches of The Seems.

Seemsian Aptitude Test (SAT): The exam used to determine one's natural affinity for a position in The Seems (1800 is a perfect score).

Slim Jim: A chewy meat by-product available in stick form at supermarkets and convenience stores in The World.

Special Commendation: An award or certificate granted to a Fixer or Briefer for exceptional performance in the line of duty.

Stream of Consciousness: Beginning in the Middle of Nowhere and bisecting Alphabet City, this tributary is believed to contain the sum experience of everyone who's ever been. Swimming is strictly prohibited, though teenagers in The Seems have been sneaking in for years.

Stumbling Block: A multitiered obstacle course designed to test the physical, emotional, and spiritual limits of Candidates at the IFR.

Sunset Strip: The back lot in the Department of Public Works where Sunset Painters prepare their daily masterworks for display.

The Tide: A revolutionary movement in The Seems bent on unseating the Powers That Be and redesigning The World.

Tool: A device/gadget used by Fixers or Briefers to complete their crucial work.

Toolkit: Any case or bag carried by Fixers containing their Tools.

Toolshed (aka Shed): The facility on the grounds of the IFR in which Fixer Tools are developed and housed.

Torch, the: Lit by Jaysun himself and protected by a small bronze censer, this flame symbolizes the unofficial leader of The Fixers. It has never been extinguished.

Train, the: An old-fashioned steam locomotive (complete with passenger and sleeping cars) that travels to the Outskirts, Beyond, Who Knows Where, and the End of the Line.

Training: The time period during which one is a Candidate at the IFR.

Twists of Fate: Small pretzel-like connectors used to affect wild changes in the Plan.

Unwilling, the: An intransigent group of naysayers who meet on a regular basis, usually to issue "Disagreements"—dense treatises decrying this, that, or the other thing.

Violation: The breaking of any Seemsian Rule.

Who Knows Where: A small settlement on the border of Seemsberia and the Middle of Nowhere, populated by exiles, unauthorized Hope prospectors, and other unsavory elements.

Window: A screen, TV, or flat-panel LCD used to monitor goings-on in The World.

Winds of Change: Powerful gusts of magnetic energy that are known to sweep across the In-Between, sometimes causing wild paradigm shifts in The World.

The World: An ambitious project in The Seems whose stated intention is to create "the most amazing, magical realm possible."

Another Story

It's not a glamorous story, but it is the way it happened.

Back in the Day, the people who lived in The Seems didn't really have a name for it. If they had to call it something, they called it "Here," and when the idea for The World came up, they just called that "There." And then there was everything "In-Between." Anyway, while The World was still in preproduction, a few of the Powers That Be decided that these names were boring and not reflective of the magical qualities that they were trying to represent. Hence, the Naming Convention was held to try to sort this mess out.

The World was named The World in short order (that's Another Story 2), but deciding on the name of the place where they worked and lived plunged the entire assembly into a fierce debate. Some wanted to call it "The Other Side," others "The Backdrop," and still others something "more fantasy/sci-fi" like "Zebulon" or "Planet X," but these were all shot down. Finally, a group of moderates suggested "The Seams," based on the seams in the newly woven Fabric of Reality, through which people could move back and forth between the worlds. This garnered a fair amount of support, but still felt a little flat, until the Original Artist (a humble painter tasked with designing the look and feel of both sides) remarked, "Why don't we call it The Seems?"

It didn't quite make sense, and there was some concern about the spelling and whether anyone would get it, but everyone agreed it had a certain "trippy" quality about it (which they liked) as well as some actual relevance and double entendre. Over the course of the lunch break, various factions began to coalesce around this initiative, and by five o'clock Happy Hour (when Cups of Cheer were handed out), it was all but a fait accompli.

Occasionally, there are still calls for a second Naming Convention, but given the amount of letterhead, signage, and popular support for the current monikers, most authorities on the subject believe that train has already left the station.

Tools of the Trade

Selected Tools from "The Glitch in Sleep." (*Note*: Reprinted from *The Catalog*, copyright © Seemsbury Press, MCGBXVII, The Seems.)

Tool Name: Blinker™
Use: Communication. While older series featured only "call-in" functionality, newer titanium models include access to FixerNet and Mission Dbase, as well as Mission Simulation mode.
Designer: Al Penske

Tool Name: Me-2™
Use: Named "Tool of the Year" for the sixth consecutive season, the Me-2 provides the ultimate in cover. Employing "youplicate" technology, the Me-2 inflates to a perfect replica of its owner and adjusts to any and all situations.
Designer: Al Penske

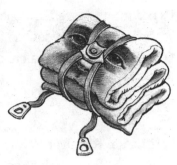

Tool Name: Sprecheneinfaches™ (spréck-en-ein-fack-ess)
Use: Universal language translator. Fluent in every known language (including Plant and Animal). Affixes to the tongue via polyurethane sheath.
Designer: Klaus van Barrelhaus

Tool Name: Glitchometer™
Use: Tracking Glitches. Retired due to design flaws that surfaced in "Clean Sweep," Glitchometers are no longer manufactured, but they can often be found on the Black or Gray markets. Handle with care.
Designer: Jayson

Tool Name: Toolmaster 3000™
Use: With its "Inverted Space Technology" (IST), the Toolmaster 3000 redefines "state of the art." Carries up to 500 items. Includes Velcro straps; triple stitched for comfort.
Designer: Al Penske

Tool Name: Receiver™
Use: Intra-Seems telephony. Now available in blue, black, Guide Gold, and traditional orange.
Designer: The Handyman

Tool Name: Time Piece™
Use: Accurate Seems–World Time reflection. Available at fine Second Hand Stores everywhere. (Requires one BBB battery, not included.)
Designer: Department of Time

Tool Name: Transport Goggles™
Use: Eyewear specifically created for In-Between travel. Features No-fog lenses®. Also jacks into Blinker for use in VR applications.
Designer: The Handyman

Tool Name: Trouble Gum™
Use: Available in cherry, grape, old-fashioned bubble, and flavorless flavors. Delivers calm in the toughest Fixing spots—a must-have.
Designer: Al Penske

Tool Name: A Breath of Fresh Air™
Use: Resuscitation. When properly used, this tool clears the lungs and gives you a whole new lease on life.
Designer: Al Penske

Tool Name: Concrete Galoshes™
Use: "Never leave home without 'em!" These boots provide added weight for light-hearted or lack-of-gravity situations. Steel-toe reinforced, made from 100% stone-milled cinder.
Designer: The Handyman

Tool Name: Those Things That Look a Lot Like Tweezers That You Cut Wires With™
Use: Pinching, biting, grabbing, twisting, stabbing, cutting, snipping, clamping, cocktail party conversation.
Designer: Al Penske

Tool Name: Pajamas™
Use: Specific to the Department of Sleep, Pajamas are your hazmat solution source. Protects against Sleep,

Hot Flashes, Bad Vibes, et al. In-store only.
Designer: Department of Sleep

Tool Name: Bed Bug Repellent™
Use: The pet project of Briefer Milton Frye, Ret., this repellent temporarily renders Bed Bugs (and many others) incapacitated for 7–9 sms. Available upon request.
Designer: Milton Frye

Tool Name: Jayson's Invention™
Use: All.
Designer: Jayson
Note: Clearance 9/9+ required. Please allow 4–6 weeks for delivery.

Tool Name: The Helping Hand (patent pending)
Use: Snatching things from relative distances. First used in "The Glitch in Sleep." Available Winter MGBJUIKK.
Designer: Fixer
F. Becker Drane

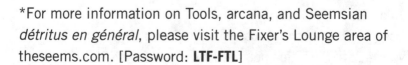

*For more information on Tools, arcana, and Seemsian *détritus en général*, please visit the Fixer's Lounge area of theseems.com. [Password: **LTF-FTL**]

Form #**1030**
Post Mission Report

Mission: The Glitch in Sleep [037001]

Filed by: F. Becker Drane

Summary:

All in all, I would say that the Glitch in Sleep went pretty well. There were a few minor Blunders on my part, but thankfully I was able to recover and, using proper techniques, complete the Mission at hand. I had fun doing it, per Fixing 302, and ultimately The World was saved and Sleep restored to said persons. Despite the Degree of Difficulty involved, it was a great first Mission for me and I am proud to have gone on it.

Areas for Improvement:

Well, there was one small, minor mistake, which we don't have to get into any further, but I would say following the Rules a little more closely would probably be a good idea for me next time. Unless they have to be broken, of course.

Rate Your Briefer (1–12): _10_

Simly performed extremely well during the Mission and I would recommend him highly to any other Fixer, as well as

possibly to be considered for promotion someday.
Confidence still an issue.

Suggestions Box:

I know everyone complains about this, but it would be
really great if we could get better Receiver reception
within The Seems. Maybe a Fixer or a Mechanic could be
assigned to add another tower or increase the amplitude
of the existing one? Also, this might not be the place to
talk about it, but I was thinking maybe we should change
the Rotation system to be less random and more tailored
to whoever is right for the job. That way someone with
experience with Glitches might have gotten this one,
instead of me. (Not that I'm complaining.)

$\checkmark$ Check here if you are interested in volunteering for
the annual Food for Thought fund drive.

F. Becker Drane Signature

Human Resources

Dear Friend:

Thank you for your interest in The Seems!

As you may or may not know, positions in The Seems occasionally come open for qualified persons in The World. Fixer, of course, is one of our most popular offerings, but there are countless other jobs (full and part time) that are essential to the smooth running of both sides.

Whether catching the Breeze or checking your local pond or lake for proper Shimmer is your cup of tea, we invite you to fill out an SAT (Seemsian Aptitude Test) at our Web site, theseems.com.

Even if we can't fulfill your employment request at this time, we keep a large file of completed SATs on hand. After all, you never know when you might be called upon to chip in for the cause.

Again, thank you for your interest in The Seems and have a great day!

Best regards,

Nick Dejanus

Nick Dejanus

Associate Director, Human Resources

Everyone Who Believed:

Jennifer Altman, Eleanor Altman, Ross Baker, Eric Bergner, the Bratters, Caroline Burfield, Becca Chapman, Evelyn Chapman, Samantha Dareff, Sandy & Harvey Dareff, Debbie & Albie, Hadley Eure, Henry Field, Todd Field, Terrapin Frazier, Ellen Hulme, Jack Ronald Hulme, David Kuhn, Rose Laurano, Julia Lazarus, Adam Levine, Elliott & Simon Liebling, Brian Lipson, Andy Liebau, Aly Mandel, Bob Marcus, Tift Merritt, John Morisano, Tim Nye, Ken Park, Julie Pepito, Ted Pryde, Carol Sawdye, Liz Schonhorst, Lucille Schulman, Deb Shapiro, Greg Siegel, Tony Gaenslen, Kenyata Sullivan, the Watermans, Victoria Wells Arms, Ann Wexler, Ari Wexler, Jamie Wexler, Philip, Ilene, Helen, Ava, Amy & Alex, and Bill & Susan. Everyone who believed but we forgot to mention they believed.

And of course, Becker Drane.